BLINDSIDED

USA TODAY & WALL STREET JOURNAL BESTSELLING AUTHOR

BECCA STEELE

AUTHOR'S NOTE

The author is British, and this story contains British English spellings and phrases. The football referred to in this story is known as soccer in some countries.

Enjoy!

For Evelyn

All it takes is a second and your whole life can get turned upside down.

JODI PICOULT, *SALEM FALLS*

NOAH

PAST

"Suck me off, Stephens."

Kyle Sanderson, the school football team captain, leaned back against the wall of the science block with his arms folded across his chest.

From my position on my knees on the tarmac, I glanced up at him with a raised brow. "Ask me nicely."

He let out an irritated huff of breath. "I'll return the fucking favour, okay? I'll give you a handjob if you just fucking hurry up."

"Yeah, alright." As I lowered my head, I promised myself this would be the last time. He'd never even kissed me. Refused to, in fact. This "thing" consisted of occasional rushed blowjobs and handjobs with a guy that was so in denial that I was almost certain he pretended I was a girl when I touched him. He always kept his eyes closed the entire time, and I was positive I'd heard him say "Daisy" once or twice when I was getting him off—which was the name of one of the most popular girls in our school.

1

This was not what I wanted for myself. Of course, I wasn't going to push anyone to come out or anything like that, but that wasn't what this was about. I knew I was no more than a willing hand-slash-mouth to him, a secret thrill to be indulged in when he felt like it, and the rest of the time, he acted like I didn't even exist.

I was worth more than that, yet I always seemed to cave whenever he texted me, and I hated that I did so easily. Generally, I was happy in myself, and I'd never hidden the fact that I was gay. Not only that, but I had the best fucking family in the world who loved and supported me unconditionally. And yet here I was, running to Kyle again as soon as he'd texted me. He was gorgeous, no doubt about it, but nothing real could ever come of this...whatever this thing was between us.

I shook my head as sudden clarity speared through me.

I deserved better than this.

And that meant this had to end here. Right now.

Gathering all my determination and courage, I raised my head, looking back up at him. His eyes were already screwed shut, and it took him a minute to realise that I wasn't doing what he wanted.

Finally, his eyes opened, and he stared at me impatiently. "What are you doing?"

I climbed to my feet, meeting his gaze. "What I should have done after the first time this happened. I don't want to do this anymore, Kyle."

He stared at me for a second, his mouth falling open before he recovered. "Yeah? What's the problem? Too good to suck my dick now, huh?"

"No, I just think I deserve better," I said honestly. "I don't like this sneaking around, waiting for the crumbs of attention you throw my way."

His eyes narrowed. "Is this because I don't want to kiss you? I told you, it's not like that. This is about getting off, nothing more. Do I need to remind you that I'm straight?"

No, because you remind me almost every time we do this. I counted to three in my head before I replied, "Everything you've just said only reinforces my decision." Thankfully, my voice remained steady.

His gaze lowered, hiding his expression from me, and I saw his jaw clench. When he raised his head again, his eyes were hard. He laughed mirthlessly. "Fuck you, Stephens. Like you could do any better." Before I could respond, he continued. "If you ever breathe a word of what happened between us, your life won't be worth living."

Then he shoved past me, sending me crashing into the wall, and he was gone. I exhaled a shaky breath. In my mind, I knew I'd done the right thing, and I'd always held back to protect myself, never allowing myself to even think about imagining anything more with him, because I knew that it would never happen. But that didn't stop it hurting.

───────

I spent the rest of the day alternating between being proud of myself for finally saying no to Kyle and feeling sad that it was over. Logically, I had no doubt I'd made the right decision; it would just take a while for the rest of my brain to catch up. I just needed to get out of here, back to the comfort and safety of my home, surrounded by the people who loved me most.

When the final bell rang to mark the end of the school day, therefore marking the end of a torturous hour of P.E., I wasted no time in getting off the playing field and making a run for the gym changing room door. Consequently, I wasn't paying attention to where I was going, and the breath was suddenly punched from my lungs when I rebounded straight off someone's body.

"Where are you going, gay boy?"

"What's the matter? Too much of a wimp to play football? Yeah, I saw you hiding in the corner doing fuck all while the rest of us did all the hard work." Mike and Scott, two members of the football team, sneered down at me as they blocked the entrance to the gym.

I gritted my teeth. I knew that it was wisest not to engage with them, but before I knew it, my mouth was flying open. "Maybe I have better things to do with my time than kick a piece of inflated leather around a field."

The hard push came from behind me, and I stumbled, my hand flying out to the wall to balance myself. The second I'd regained my balance, I spun around, my fists clenched. Three of the other football players stood there, smirking at me.

"Don't fucking touch me." I glared at them, daring them to try anything else.

"Stephens."

Kyle. I groaned under my breath as the last person I wanted to see swaggered over to his teammates, all cocky confidence as he drew closer to his friends. Yet, there was a flash of something that looked a lot like remorse in his gaze as he looked at me, but he covered it quickly.

Mike's gaze returned to me, and he narrowed his eyes. He opened his mouth, no doubt to say something cutting, but was stopped by Kyle placing a hand on his arm. "Leave it, Mike. People like him will never get it."

"Loser," Mike hissed as he shoved past me, heading into the changing room with his teammates, leaving me fuming in their wake.

As soon as this final school year was over, I was getting away from this place, and I couldn't wait to leave. Yeah, I'd miss my family, a lot, but it wasn't like I couldn't come back and visit them. London was only a couple of hours away, after all.

The benefits would be more than worth it. No more having to deal with the popular football players swaggering around, acting like complete wankers to anyone who wasn't interested in their sport. No more whispered comments behind my back. No more narrow-minded people, the same faces I saw day in, day out. No more secrets.

No more football.

A fresh start, in a new city.

I couldn't wait.

Less than a year to go.

ONE

NOAH

I rounded a corner, and there it was.

London Southwark University. My home for the next three years.

As I drove past the first of the LSU campus buildings, all modern glass and steel brightly reflecting the morning sun, I couldn't stop the grin overtaking my face. Following the signs for student parking, I swung my grey Volkswagen Golf into the large car park, spotting a space all the way down the end of the left-hand side.

Perfect. I put my foot down on the pedal, speeding up to reach the space before anyone else got there.

Everything happened in slow motion.

Another VW Golf appeared from the bottom of the car park, aiming straight for my space. I slammed my foot down on the brakes too late, and the crunch of metal sounded as my car came to a sudden stop, then jerked backwards.

Fuck.

I jumped out of my car, slamming the door behind me. "What the hell? You could see I was aiming for that space!"

The other driver rounded the side of his car, yanking his

sunglasses from his eyes as he glared at me. "You drove your fucking car into mine! Are you blind?"

"It was *my* space; I already had my indicator on. Maybe you should try using your eyes for once!"

He gave an angry growl. "I was indicating too, and not only that, I was closer to the space. It was mine!" He gestured to his passenger door, which now held a sizeable dent where my car had hit it. "I'm not losing my insurance no-claims bonus for this shit. You're paying to fix it."

Breathing deeply through my nose, I attempted to curb my anger. This was not how I wanted my first day at uni to go. "Yeah? Are you gonna pay for mine?"

"Your what?" Jabbing his finger in the direction of my front bumper, he curled his lip. "That's just a fucking scratch!"

I eyed my bumper. There were long scratches across the front, but I could probably cover them with a touch-up pen. I wanted to go through the insurance route even less than he did, probably. It wasn't only my no-claims bonus on the line, the insurance excess alone would cost more than it would to fix it myself. And money was something I was in very short supply of at the moment.

I became aware of him seething at my side, and I tilted my head, studying the large dent in his door. My car had definitely come out of this better than his. A flare of sudden guilt had me opening my mouth. "I can knock the dent out if you want. It's easy enough. I've done it on my car before."

He stepped right up to me, pushing his chest into mine, and I had a sudden flashback to my school days, when the football boys used to throw their weight around as an intimidation tactic.

Too bad for him I wasn't a pushover. I shoved back against him, and his gorgeous blue eyes widened in surprise.

No. He does not have gorgeous eyes.

"I'm not surprised that you've done it to your own car, based on your lack of driving skills, but do you seriously think I'd let you come near my car again?" he continued to rant, quickly over the surprise of me pushing him back.

"Mate, we've got the same car," I pointed out, my anger receding as he got more worked up. Especially since my car seemed to have escaped mostly unscathed, other than the scratches to the bumper.

He ran a frustrated hand through his brown hair, his nostrils flaring. "Not the same," he bit out. "This is a GTI, and do you know how much the paint job was?"

I rolled my eyes. "No, and I don't particularly care. Look, it won't take me long to bang the dent out. It'll look as good as new when I'm done with it."

"You're not coming near my car. You blindsided me; it's 100 percent your fault. Pay up, or I'll get campus security involved. There's cameras all around this car park." Turning away, he reached through his open window, then spun back to face me. "I want your number, and I want you to text me right now to prove it's real, in case you do a runner."

I pulled my phone from my pocket with a sigh. "Fine. What's your number?"

He yanked my phone from my grip, his nostrils flaring with anger.

"Seriously." I rolled my eyes at him. Again. "You need to calm down."

While he was occupied with jabbing at my phone, I took a chance to take him in properly. He was taller than me but not by much, with a fairly lean build. Although his body was hidden under his hoodie, I'd bet anything, based on the way his jeans clung to his muscled thighs, that he'd be ripped. His mid-brown hair was shot through with naturally sun-kissed highlights—the kind that appeared after a long, hot summer spent outside. It was kind of longish and messy on the top of his head but short around the sides, with a line shaved into the right side. But it was his face that stopped me in my tracks—fucking gorgeous with aqua-blue eyes tipped with long chestnut lashes, a strong jawline with the barest hint of stubble, and full lips. All in all, he was the kind of boy that got my heart racing and my dick hard.

There was no doubt that he was very, very hot, but it was more or less negated by the fact that, based on first impressions, he was a complete and utter bellend.

When he was done with trying to stab his fingers through my phone screen, he thrust my phone back at me and then climbed back into his car without another word. The next second, there was the sound of his engine roaring to life.

"Hang on." I strode over and leaned down, poking my head through the open passenger window. "Don't you want to exchange names?"

"No need." He brandished his phone at me, baring his teeth. "I have you listed under 'Car Park Wanker.'"

"How sweet. We already have nicknames for each other." I gave him a fake smile before withdrawing my head from his car.

"Wait, what's your nickname for me?" he called out.

I ignored his question just to annoy him even more. "See you around."

With another fake smile, I sauntered away, sliding behind the wheel of my car and giving him a mock salute, before reversing away and finding another space in the car park, as far away from him as possible.

TWO

NOAH

By the time I found myself standing outside my new student house, my mood had improved. Close to the LSU campus, it was a large, white-painted Victorian terrace with bay windows. From the information I'd received from the housing coordinator, the row of houses on this street was collectively known as "the Mansions," identical Victorian three-storey terraced buildings that housed students from the university.

Pressing my finger to the tarnished doorbell next to the black-painted door, below a brass number three, I shifted on my feet, sudden nerves overtaking me. I'd spoken to Gary, one of the LSU housing coordinators, a number of times, and I'd sent all my stuff ahead of me other than the bag I was currently holding. He'd assured me that my new house-mates would welcome me, but in all honesty, his words didn't mean anything. I was about to move into a house with complete strangers, and it was my first time being away from my mum, dad, and my thirteen-year-old twin sisters, Layla and Ami.

The heavy wooden door swung open, interrupting my

thoughts. A tall blond guy stood in the doorway, his brows rising as I stared at him in silence.

I cleared my throat. *Stop being so fucking nervous.* "Sorry. Hi? I mean, Hi. I'm Noah. Noah Stephens. I'm moving in?"

His face relaxed into a genuine smile, and he held out a hand in greeting. "Hey, man. We've been expecting you. It's good to meet you. I'm Preston."

"You're not English," I said, stating the obvious and immediately wishing my brain-to-mouth filter was working.

He laughed, glancing back at me over his shoulder as I followed him into the wide hallway, complete with black-and-white chequered tiles. "Nope. American. Come on in."

I followed him into the room to our left, which was a large lounge, complete with three sagging grey sofas, exposed wooden floors, and a giant TV with a gaming console. A pine dining table with six chairs stood at the far end of the room in front of a door that looked like it led out into a courtyard garden, and a battered coffee table with an ashtray and a couple of empty glasses was the only other piece of furniture I could see.

"Guys. This is Noah. He's moving in today."

Three sets of eyes turned to stare at me. My cheeks warmed, but I kept my composure. Preston came to stand by my side, and I appreciated his silent support.

"Uh, hi."

Preston took over again, seeming to sense my nerves. "Okay. This is Ander. He lives next door at number 1, but he's here all the time." He pointed to a broad-shouldered, good-looking guy with his feet kicked up on the coffee table. He smiled at me, and I returned the gesture.

"And over here...this is my boyfriend, Kian, who doesn't live here either." At the mention of his name, Kian raised his head. He had intense light green eyes, dark hair, and a kind of bad-boy aura that not many guys could pull off successfully, in my opinion. His lip piercing glinted as his mouth curved into a small smile.

Wait. "Your boyfriend?" What were the chances of me ending up in a place with gay housemates? Suddenly, I was a lot more relaxed.

Pausing to glance back at me, Preston smiled cautiously. "Yeah..."

"That's great. I mean, I'm gay. So it's good to have, you know. Support." I could feel my cheeks flush, but I held his gaze.

His smile widened, his blue eyes sparkling. "I knew I liked you." Leaning closer to me, he lowered his voice conspiratorially. "There's a really good gay club I discovered last semester, if you're interested in that kind of thing. I'm gonna try and drag Kian there one of these days, and I might need some help convincing him."

Out of the corner of my eye, I could see Kian watching us with an amused look on his face as I nodded. "Yeah, that sounds good to me. Count me in."

"Cool." He cleared his throat and threw out his arm in the direction of the only guy in the room that I hadn't been introduced to yet. "Last but not least, meet one of your actual housemates, Travis."

My gaze swept over Travis' dark hair and grinning face. He gave me a casual nod, lifting his hand in greeting. I returned his nod with a smile.

Preston stepped back towards the doorway. "So that's everyone here right now. I guess you'll meet our other housemates, Liam and Damon, later. Damon's in his first year, same as you. As for Liam and Travis here, they're both in their second year, same as me—"

"And Trav's the dad of your house," Ander interjected with a grin. Travis leaned across the sofas to punch him in the arm.

"Fuck off. I told you not to call me that."

Ander grinned at him unrepentantly. "You love it, mate."

Preston shook his head at their antics. "Trav's the oldest, in case you couldn't tell."

He continued talking as we headed out of the lounge, and he showed me into a large kitchen, complete with another pine table, this one with bench seats, and another door leading to the small yard. Across the hallway from the lounge, there was a room containing a load of media equipment—cameras, lights, a backdrop on a stand, and what looked like a sound deck. After I'd briefly peered into the room, Preston swung the door closed. "Travis is doing a media degree, and his girlfriend, Kira, is doing a photography degree. All their very expensive equipment is in there, and it's off limits to the rest of us. On pain of death."

"Noted." We left the room behind, and I followed him up the stairs, where he showed me the three bedrooms belonging to himself, Damon, and Travis. Travis' bedroom was at the far end, away from the others—apparently soundproofed so he could work on his media projects and not be disturbed. Up the final flight of stairs, we reached the top floor and the attic bedrooms. One was Liam's, and finally, at the end of the hallway, there was mine. I'd been told it was the smallest room in the house, so I was prepared for a tiny box room.

It was a nice surprise to find out that the room wasn't as small as I'd been led to believe. Yeah, it was smallish, but it was actually bigger than my bedroom back home. At home, I had the smallest room in the house so my sisters could share the bigger bedroom. Here I had more space to spread out. There was a double bed, a small tan two-seater sofa, a desk with a small bookcase next to it, and a wardrobe with drawers at the bottom. I had my own bathroom too, as did all the bedrooms in this house.

A tiny window gave me a view mostly consisting of roofs and a sliver of sky, and the bedroom ceiling sloped on one side, but all in all, I was happy.

"This is better than I was expecting."

Preston eyed me doubtfully. "Is it? I guess I should tell you...I've been told that the pipes are noisy. They're in the wall right behind your room."

"What, like hot water pipes?"

He nodded. "Yeah, I think so."

"It's alright. I've got a white noise app—I can use that if it gets loud when I'm trying to sleep." I wasn't concerned. I had my own room, and I was at university at last. Someone had already set my computer on the desk, and my few boxes were neatly stacked in the corner of the room, ready to unpack. "This is good, honestly."

"Good. I'll leave you to get settled in, then." He paused in the doorway, giving me a smile. "Do you want to swap numbers?"

"Yeah. That'd be good. Thanks."

When he'd disappeared, I dumped my bag on the bed and got to work unpacking my boxes. Once everything was in place, I headed back downstairs and into the kitchen. I pulled up my family group chat and tapped out a message to say I'd arrived safely. That done, I explored the kitchen, discovering my allocated cupboard and fridge space in the kitchen. I placed what few items I had inside, but the shelves were still practically bare when I was done. At this point in time, I didn't have much in the way of foodstuffs.

There'd been a mix-up with my student loan, thanks to my dad's recent change in job situation, so one of my priorities was to rectify that as soon as possible.

But that was a worry for tomorrow. For now, nothing could bring down my mood. I was finally here in London, a uni student at last, and I needed to get to know my house-mates and whoever else was going to be a regular visitor here.

Ander had left by the time I made it back into the lounge.

"Wanna play?" Travis held up a PS5 controller, waving it at me. "It's a rite of passage for the new housemates."

Taking a seat next to him on the sofa, I grinned at the surprising realisation that I was already feeling at home here. "Yeah. What are we playing?"

I was completely engrossed in what was happening on the screen when the front door slammed loudly, so I barely paid the noise any attention. The game was at a crucial point, with Travis leaning forward next to me and swearing loudly at the TV as our characters ducked down behind a wall to escape the heavy fire we'd been under.

The next second, though, I heard a low, angry voice coming from the direction of the door.

"What's *he* doing here?"

The game was suddenly forgotten as my head flew up, my eyes meeting a pair of enraged blue ones.

Fuck.

The guy from the car park was here.

THREE

LIAM

"Liam, meet our new housemate, Noah."

I ignored Travis' voice, still staring over at the dark-haired guy who was lounging on *my* sofa, feet kicked up on *my* coffee table, with *my* game controller in his hand. He looked over at me, and something that might have been shock or apprehension flashed in his bright amber eyes before he quickly masked it.

Wait a fucking minute.

"Did you say housemate?"

"Yeah." Travis raised a brow at my expression, which I could tell was murderous even without a mirror. "Noah. He moved in today."

The guy, *Noah*, put his controller down and stood, crossing over to me and holding out his hand for me to shake, like he hadn't driven into my car just a few hours earlier. *Wanker.* "Hi, Liam. Nice to meet you."

Ignoring his outstretched hand, I clenched my jaw as he stood there smirking at me. But I could feel the stares of my housemates, and it was clear that Noah wanted me to cause a scene in front of them. Too bad for him I wasn't going to give him the satisfaction. So I pasted on a fake smile. "Alright, mate. Hope you're all settled in. Can I speak to you for a minute?"

The smirk was instantly wiped away, and he followed me out of the room without question. I headed into the kitchen, assuming he would follow me. When we were a safe distance from the others, I stopped, spinning to face him. "Are we gonna have a problem?" I stared him down, arms crossed over my chest.

He shot me an unimpressed look that made me bristle. "Is this about the car? That was your fault, if you recall."

"*My* fault?" My voice dropped dangerously, but he either didn't care about the threat in my tone, or he was too dense to notice it.

"That's right." Giving me a tentative grin, he shrugged. "Okay, I know I was angry at the time, but I'm over it now. And I'm taking care of the ding in your car, so no harm done."

I gaped at this delusional idiot. "It was your fucking fault. And I told you, you're not coming near my car again. Pay for my repairs, and stay out of my way in future."

"Uh, yeah, about that." His smile dropped, and he stepped back, running a hand through his tousled dark hair. "There was a mix-up in the student loans department, so I don't have the money just yet." He lowered his gaze, and his voice grew quieter. "I...uh, won't be able to afford to get food otherwise. If you refuse to let me knock out the dent myself, you'll have to wait a bit, but it should only be a week, max."

"Yeah, no. That's not gonna work for me. Pay up. I've booked the car in with the garage, so I'll give you twenty-four hours to come up with the money. Four hundred quid for the repair and paint job."

"Do you want me to starve?" Finally, his eyes darkened with anger, and I almost smiled.

"Not my problem, dickhead. Maybe it'll teach you to stop and think before you try taking someone else's space."

The fuming silence lasted for all of two seconds before the anger disappeared from his face. His gaze tracked across my body, and his tongue came out to slide over his lips. What the fuck? Was he actually standing here checking me out? "Or I could pay the debt off another way."

I jerked backwards. "Fuck. Off. I'm straight, so no, and also. *Fuck* no. Not if you were the last person on earth."

His eyes widened. Holding up his hands, he backed away from me. "What? I wasn't implying— All I meant was if you wanted any help with coursework, or chores, or whatever."

I breathed deeply through my nose, attempting to keep my control. Clearly, this guy was trying to fuck with my head and get a rise out of me. "I don't want any help with anything, especially if it comes from you. Find me the money within twenty-four hours."

Pushing past him, I stormed out of the door, taking the stairs two at a time to get up to my bedroom.

He'd been the one to run into my car, and yet he was somehow under the mistaken impression that it wasn't his fault. How the fuck had he come to that conclusion?

Fucking deluded wanker.

For a few blissful hours, I managed to forget all about my new dickhead housemate until I was rudely awakened by Travis banging on my door at some ungodly hour the following morning.

"Get up! Last day before freshers' week starts! Time to see what the new recruits are made of."

I groaned. "Have you seen the time?" I called through the door. "Come back in an hour. At least."

"No can do. I'm meeting Kira at twelve, and anyway, I booked the pitch for 8:oo a.m."

Burying my face in my pillow, I groaned again before raising my head, blinking the sleep from my eyes. "Fine. Give me a few to shower."

As I dragged myself out of bed and into my bathroom, I distantly heard him banging on another door, and then I remembered.

Fucking Noah.

He'd better be good at football. That was the only thing that could redeem him at this point.

Showered and dressed in my football kit in record time, I pulled on a sky-blue LSU hoodie and grabbed my boot bag before heading downstairs to where the others were congregating in the kitchen. Preston handed me a mug of coffee, and I leaned against the kitchen counter as I drank.

"Ready to show us what you've got?" Travis glanced between Damon and another new student, Levi, who'd just moved into the house next door, where our teammate Ander lived. "Living with us gets you an automatic advantage—we'll vouch for you when you apply to join the team, and you're more or less guaranteed a place."

"*If* you're any good," I interjected, and Travis rolled his eyes.

"They wouldn't be living here if they weren't any good. Perks of having an in with the housing coordinator, remember?"

Travis' girlfriend's family owned the rental agency that we used, and her older brother was in charge of the rooms to rent in the Mansions. He vetted the prospective students, and because we had two rooms up for grabs this year after two of the older housemates had moved out to live with their girlfriends, he'd hand-selected students who had a vested interest in football and were more or less guaranteed to get a spot on the team. Number 3 had always been a football house, and that was the way it was going to stay. It was a shame we hadn't had enough bedrooms for Levi as well, but at least he had Ander in his house.

"What's going on?" Noah, aka Car Park Wanker, wandered in, yawning and rubbing at his eyes, dressed way too casually in low-slung faded jeans and a grey T-shirt. He turned to Travis. "Sorry, I was half asleep when you knocked."

"Where's your football kit? You can't go out like that." I spoke up before Travis could reply, and he shot me an annoyed frown.

"What's your problem today? You've been in a pissed-off mood ever since yesterday."

"I wonder why." Directing a pointed glare at Noah, which caused him to scratch his chin with his middle finger, I gulped down a huge mouthful of coffee.

"Whatever. I don't have time to deal with it this morning." Travis turned his attention back to Noah. "Noah. Sorry, I forgot you weren't here when I made the announcement yesterday. We've booked the football pitch for eight. It's a chance for you freshers to show us what you can do, see where your strengths lie and all that, and it'll hopefully give you an advantage when it comes to applying to be on the team."

Noah's face paled, and his eyes widened dramatically. "Football pitch?" He whispered the words, his suddenly panicked gaze darting around the room, seemingly realising that everyone present was dressed in some variation of a football kit. "What...why would you want to see me play football?"

"To see where your strengths lie. I just told you." Now I could see that Travis was starting to get annoyed with him as well as me. I hid my smirk behind my coffee mug.

"But I don't have—I mean, I don't play football. I don't even watch it. In fact, I'd go so far as to say I hate it." His voice was rising, the agitation clear in his tone.

"Wait. You what? You don't play football? Why—" Travis cut himself off, shaking his head. "'Scuse me a minute. I need to phone Kira."

There was dead silence in the kitchen after he'd left the room, phone in hand. No one seemed to know what to say. Eventually, Preston headed over to Noah and gave his arm a squeeze. "Hey. I'm sure it's all a big misunderstanding." He studied Noah intently, then leaned against the counter next to him, speaking in a soft voice. "Why is it that you don't like soccer—uh, football? Is it personal?"

Noah chewed on his lip and then finally gave a short nod. "Yeah, I suppose it is, a bit. At school, I, uh...I was the gay kid who wasn't interested in football, and some of the players took personal offence at that...you know how it is." His tone was flat, but his gaze dropped to the floor, his long lashes sweeping down to hide his anxious expression. I could see his fists clenching and unclenching at his sides, and he was still worrying at his lip with his teeth. "I'm just not into football. At all. I never have been," he added in a quieter voice.

"You don't have to worry about any of that from us. No one here will treat you any differently—not because you don't share certain interests *or* because you're gay."

Preston's voice hardened as he glanced around the kitchen. "Right?"

"Yep." Damon gave a shrug, unbothered by the whole conversation, more interested in whatever was happening on his phone.

Levi nodded. "I guess I don't get a vote, since I'm not a housemate, but for what it's worth, I'm bi. And I wouldn't give you shit for not liking football."

"You're bi?" Preston stared at him.

"Uh, yeah. The year after you left school, when I became captain... You know our old rivals, Highnam Academy? We started some shit with them, and their team captain didn't take it too well. One thing led to another, and now...he's my boyfriend."

Preston shook his head, amusement dancing in his eyes. "Shit, man, it sounds like you've got a story to tell."

He grinned widely. "You could say that, yeah. I'll tell you later, catch you up on all the Alstone High news."

"Deal. Okay. Liam. You're up."

I sighed loudly. "You know I'm not homophobic, mate. But yeah, I do have a problem with him being here if he's not interested in football. You know this is supposed to be a house for LSU football team players—always has been. Everyone who lives here was hand-selected for their skills, and they're pretty much guaranteed a place on the team. Now we have one person fucking up that balance."

"It's really not a big deal," Preston insisted.

"Maybe not to you," I muttered. Slamming my coffee mug down on the countertop, I shot a glance at Noah. Hurt was shining in his eyes, which he quickly masked, giving me a hard glare. His lip curled, and he opened his mouth—but I didn't get to hear what he wanted to say because Travis came back into the kitchen and clapped his hands for attention.

"Okay. It appears there was a mix-up with the housing allocations. Levi—you were supposed to be here, and Noah, you were supposed to be next door. There's nothing we can do about it now, not without causing a massive fucking headache for the housing team. All the paperwork has been filed." He sighed, rubbing his hand across his face, and then turned to Noah. "Look, I know this isn't an ideal situation. But I think I speak for us all when I say this—if you're happy to stay, we're more than happy to have you. You seem like a good guy. I can't promise we won't talk about football, but we'll do our best to keep it to a minimum around you." He gave Noah a genuine smile, and the stiffness went out of Noah's shoulders. A small, hesitant smile curved over his lips, directed at Travis, and something inside me twisted.

He straightened up, some of the apprehension leaving his gaze. "Thanks. You're right—it's not an ideal situation for any of us. I—you were out of the room when I told the others that I'd had some issues with football players in the past, and I guess it's made me a bit...y'know." He shrugged, his mouth twisting. "But you guys have been nothing but welcoming to me." Right after he'd said those words, he shot me a sideways glance, and I heard his unspoken *except you*. "I'll try my hardest to be a decent housemate."

Unlikely.

Travis nodded. "We've known our fair share of asshole players too, but I promise that none of us here are like that." He glanced over at me with a smirk. "That includes Liam. He's just a grumpy bastard at the moment."

I glared at him, but he'd already turned back to Noah. "Now that's all been said, let me officially welcome you to number 3, housemate."

They grinned at each other.

This couldn't be happening.

"How the fuck can this be happening?"

"Seriously, Liam, what's your problem? You're really starting to piss me off now." Travis shot me a warning look.

Oh. I said that aloud. And fuck Travis. He might be the oldest person here, but he had no right to act like he was in charge of us.

Except, yeah...he was our team captain. I probably shouldn't piss him off too much, otherwise he'd bench me just to make a point. "Alright. Sorry, okay? I'm...fuck, I don't know. Tired and shit."

He raised his brows, nodding in the direction of Noah. "It's not just me you should be apologising to."

"Fine. I apologise to anyone I might have annoyed or offended or whatever. Happy?"

"No, but it'll have to do. I don't have time for this. Come on, we're gonna be late if we don't get a move on." He began herding us out of the door, stopping to speak in Noah's ear, too low for me to catch. Noah gave him another small smile, then leaned back against the countertop with his arms folded across his chest. For someone that allegedly had an aversion to sports, he seemed to be very fucking well defined. I straightened my shoulders, flexing my muscles deliberately as I crossed the room, and he snorted, amused.

"See you later, *housemate*." A wide, fake smile appeared on his face, showing his straight, white teeth in all their glory.

"Fuck you." I flipped him the finger, and he returned the gesture, his fake smile morphing into a genuine grin.

Wanker.

FOUR

LIAM

The student union bar was mostly full of first years since it was freshers' week. Travis and Ander had dragged all the housemates from number 1 and 3 out to induct our newbies into student life or some shit. Preston was playing doubles pool with Damon and two of the guys from the football team. Travis, Ander, and Ander's best mate, Elliot, were crowded around the fruit machines, watching their friend JJ's failed attempt to win money. That left me standing at the bar on babysitter duty with Levi and my new least favourite person, Noah.

We were waiting for drinks, and since I was in the middle, it was easy enough to angle my body so I had my back to Noah.

Casting around for something to say to Levi before Noah could jump in, I threw out the first question that came into my head. "Levi. What made you choose LSU?"

The next thing I knew, Noah had moved around me, and half of his body was pressed against my side. What the actual fuck? His attention was on Levi, but I knew he had to be aware of what he was doing.

The line of heat down my body felt...I couldn't even say, but he needed to get the fuck away from me, right now. I twisted to the side so he stumbled, which brought a smile to my face. "Stay out of my personal space," I hissed before turning back to Levi.

There was a long pause while Levi stared between Noah and me, his brows pulled together. The silence was finally broken by the bartender bringing our drinks over, and he seemed to shake himself out of the stupor he'd fallen into. "It was an easy decision in the end. I'm from Alstone, down on the south coast, and most of the students I went to school with ended up at Alstone College. But I want to design cars eventually, and being here in London gives me the most opportunities." A smile curved over his lips. "Plus, my boyfriend lives in London now too, and I want to be close to him. He's training to be a football coach. He gets his accommodation provided as part of the training course, but it's only a single room, otherwise I'd probably be living with him already."

Noah shifted on his feet, knocking my shoulder and making beer splash out of my pint glass and onto my T-shirt. *Fucker.* "You and me both—the opportunities part, that is. I'd like the boyfriend part too, though." He shot Levi a genuine grin that had me gritting my teeth for some reason.

"It'll happen," Levi assured him. Before I could make what probably would have been an ill-advised comment, he suddenly seemed to remember that I was still there, and he turned to me. "What about you, Liam? Why LSU?"

I shrugged. "Dunno, really. I thought it was as good a place as any. I grew up in south London, and I didn't want to go too far." I didn't add that I'd been worried about my mum being left alone...which she was until a couple of months after I'd started uni, when she'd told me about her new relationship.

I'd moved into the Mansions last September along with Travis. We already knew each other from playing on the same local youth football team for the previous three years, which had made the transition to university easier. Then I'd met our neighbour, Ander, on the day of the try-outs for the LSU football team, and we'd instantly hit it off. Gradually, my circle of friends had widened, and I'd settled into uni life with ease. I'd even stayed here over the summer instead of going home, mostly because although my mum was under an hour's drive away, or half that if I got the train, she had her new "boyfriend," and I wasn't ready to see them together just yet. I was happy for her, though. I *was*.

After taking a swig of my pint, I returned my attention to the conversation. "It's been alright here, for the most part. I had a falling-out with one of the guys on the football team last semester—he was a complete bellend, but he's graduated now. Everyone else has been great, though, other than a couple of the lecturers who seem to exist just to give us a hard time."

"Imagine *you* falling out with someone," the wanker standing next to Levi said, giving me the fakest smile I'd ever seen.

"Yeah, imagine." I shot him an equally fake smile. "I'm easy to get on with, unless I'm unfairly provoked."

His eyes narrowed.

Levi stared between us, his brows raised. "What's going on between the two of you?"

"Nothing." Noah lifted his glass to his lips, keeping his gaze on me.

Levi dropped it. "If you say so. I'm going to find Preston, then. Have fun with...whatever this is."

Locked in our silent stand-off, neither of us watched him leave.

Noah was the first to look away, dropping his gaze to his pint. That made me smile.

He downed his drink, then slammed his pint glass on the bar top with a glare. "What?"

I shrugged. What could I say without sounding like a dickhead? *Oh, I was smiling because you looked away first.* Yeah, I wasn't going to tell him that. "Nothing that concerns you," I said aloud.

His amber eyes bored into me, fringed by long, dark lashes. Who had eyes like that, anyway? They were way too fucking pretty to be wasted on a guy like him.

I recoiled at my own thoughts, my lip curling in disgust. Who the fuck cared what his fucking eyes looked like?

He caught my look and rolled said eyes at me. "Let me guess. You're still thinking about how it's supposedly my fault that I knocked into your precious car." He accompanied the words "my fault" with obnoxious air quotes.

Clenching my jaw, I counted to five under my breath before I responded. "It *was* your fault. But I'm not wasting my breath on discussing it with you anymore, when you clearly can't see that you're in the wrong."

Closing his eyes briefly, he exhaled heavily, then gave a jerky nod. "Fine." There was a second's pause, then he said, "Want a game of pool?"

He looked as surprised by the question as I was, like he hadn't meant to ask me.

"Why the fuck would I want to play with you?" I bit out before I could think my words through.

His gaze shuttered, the light going out of his eyes. Without another word to me, he pushed through the crowds and headed out of the exit door.

I shook off the unexpected spike of...whatever it was. Probably irritation that he'd run out like a coward instead of answering back. Deliberately facing the opposite way to the exit, I scanned the crowd for my friends. Ander was still over by the fruit machines, watching Elliot's attempt at winning the jackpot, so I wandered over to join him.

"Alright, mate." I greeted him with a nod, which he returned. "Tell me you got economics on Monday mornings too."

He rolled his eyes. "Yeah. First thing on a Monday morning? Whoever does the timetables is a sadist."

"Yep. Total sadist." We both laughed. Then, changing the subject, I indicated my head towards the pool table, which was now free. "Wanna play?"

"Depends. Are you prepared to have your ass kicked by the pool king?"

"You wish, mate." I shook my head at him with a grin. "Get ready to lose."

We ended up playing three games before I was distracted by the sight of a pretty girl standing at the bar, close to Travis, who was buying a pint. Long, dark brown hair and a tight, sexy ass. Just my type. I said a general goodbye to the table, nodding in the girl's direction, and Ander gave me a discreet thumbs up. We had a routine by now, after a year of being friends, with the same goal in mind. He was my wingman, and I was his. He leaned over to me, speaking in a low murmur. "Good luck, mate. She's fit as fuck. Send her blonde friend my way."

I caught Travis' eye as I glanced at the girl's friend, and he shook his head at me with a smirk. He seemed to find the way Ander and I hooked up with different girls every time amusing, for some reason. Just because he was loved-up with his girlfriend and none of the girls I pulled held my interest, didn't mean that anything was missing. He kept telling us that when we found "the one" we'd feel differently, but one: I couldn't imagine that happening, and two: I wasn't interested in it happening. My uni days were about having a good time, getting my degree, and playing football —not necessarily in that order.

"I'm on it." I clapped Ander on the back and headed over to the girl.

FIVE

NOAH

My phone alarm woke me at 8:00 a.m., and I stretched, disorientated for a second, before I remembered where I was. My bedroom in my new house.

The events of the previous day came back to me in a rush, and I lay back with a groan. When I'd first walked into the kitchen yesterday morning and been confronted by the fact that I'd somehow ended up living my worst nightmare —surrounded by a load of football players—I'd been filled with a sick dread. It had lasted most of the day, even though everyone had been quick to reassure me that they didn't think any less of me, and I was still welcome in the house. Everyone except Liam, that was, but that was no surprise. He'd managed to piss me off last night at the student union too, and I'd stormed out. It wasn't a move I was proud of, but it was probably for the best anyway—I shouldn't be out buying drinks when I knew I had to pay Liam for his car repairs.

Pulling on a pair of loose grey shorts, I stepped out of my room, yawning widely. Before anything else, even a shower, I needed coffee.

As I reached Liam's door, I had to jump backwards to avoid walking into a girl who'd just emerged from his room. "Sorry," I automatically apologised, waiting for her to go ahead of me. It looked like Liam had managed to get lucky last night, then.

My stomach twisted—an irrational, unwanted reaction. *Very* unwanted.

The girl looked me up and down with an appreciative smile. Licking her lips, she stepped closer. "Nothing to apologise for. Especially not when you look like that."

Before I could respond, the door opened again, and this time, Liam appeared, all sleepy and gorgeous, dressed similarly to me in just a pair of loose shorts, his tanned, sculpted body on display. *Fuck.* My dick liked the view far too much. I quickly moved around them both before either of them noticed, but Liam's voice stopped me in my tracks. Even his morning voice sounded sexy, a low rasp that went straight to my dick, increasing my current problem.

"Really? You're hitting on her?"

Without turning around, I threw over my shoulder, "I'm only into dick, so, no." Then I legged it downstairs before I got into another war of words with my housemate.

I stopped in the lounge before I headed into the kitchen, making a point to say hi to Travis and Preston. I was still a little unsure of my standing in this house, after finding out that my housemates were all footballers and they'd expected that I was too, but I wanted to put the effort in. My school experiences with Kyle and his teammates were relegated to my past, and now it was time to look forward to my future. No one here had done anything to make me uncomfortable yet, and if they could treat me normally, like they had done so far, maybe it was time for me to start letting go of my prejudices about football players.

That done, I made my way into the kitchen and helped myself to instant coffee from the communal tin, dumping a spoonful into a sky-blue mug branded with the LSU crest. While I waited for the kettle to boil, I logged into my online bank account to check my balance, then texted Liam. Might as well give it one last try, even though I knew it would piss him off. A small smile tugged at my lips at the thought. I didn't know what it was about him that made me keep pushing for a reaction from him, but I'd be lying if I said I didn't enjoy it in a way.

Me: Have you reconsidered letting me bang the dent out of your car? I'm great with my hands

I saw the notification to say he'd seen it, but he didn't reply. He was probably too busy with that girl.

Ignoring the tiny sting of jealousy in my chest, I poured the hot water from the kettle into my mug and gave it a stir. Instant coffee wasn't my favourite, but my options were limited at this point. At least I only had a week until my student loan came in, hopefully.

Opening the fridge, I bypassed my empty shelf and grabbed a carton of semi-skimmed milk from the door. Liam's name was written on the front in black Sharpie. I paused, thinking for a minute. He owed me, both for putting me in this situation where I had to pay him what little money I had, plus all the digs he'd been making at me. Like just a few minutes ago. Who the fuck would try hitting on a housemate's one-night stand the very next morning? Maybe some guys would, but I would never stoop that low. Fuck him for daring to suggest it. With that thought in mind, I helped myself to his milk, then found his food cupboard and took two of his slices of bread to put in the toaster.

A throat cleared as I was closing his cupboard door, making me jump. "What are you doing? That's my food cupboard."

I twisted around to see Liam leaning against the doorjamb, his eyes narrowed at me suspiciously. The girl was nowhere in sight.

"Just checking out the kitchen," I said innocently, opening and closing a few more doors at random. He looked far from convinced, but he stepped into the kitchen, helping himself to a mug and popping a coffee pod into the machine on the countertop. I took a sip of my instant coffee, trying my hardest to ignore the rich aroma of his drink.

I should've made tea instead of coffee. Or helped myself to one of Liam's pods.

My toast popped up, so I busied myself with that, using a sliver of the butter from the dish that was sitting out on the side. An uncomfortable silence fell between us as we did our best to ignore each other, but when I took a seat at the kitchen table, he sat down with me.

I stared at him in shock, but before I could say anything, he slid his phone across the table. "Here. These are my bank details. You can pay me now."

Oh. *That* was why he was sitting with me. I took my time chewing my mouthful of toast before I replied. Every second I kept him waiting, his jaw tightened even further. "You're really precious about your car, huh?" I said eventually, watching with satisfaction as he ground his teeth. How was it that he looked good even when he was all wound up and directing his anger at me?

"Money," he bit out. As he spoke, he shifted on the bench, and his leg brushed against mine.

I tried my hardest to ignore the sudden heat that shot through me, instead focusing very hard on the fact that I was annoyed with him.

"Are you sure—"

His leg pressed against mine, harder. Did he think it would intimidate me? Because it was having the opposite effect, and my dick was starting to take notice of his proximity. "Don't even fucking *think* about suggesting that you knock out the dent again. You pay me, right now, and then we never have to deal with each other again. You stay out of my way, and I'll stay out of yours."

"Okay, okay." Sliding away from him before my dick got the wrong idea about having a hot boy pressed up against me, I picked up my phone and logged back into my bank account. I input the details from his phone, then shoved my phone in his face to show him the confirmation screen. "There. It's done. Happy now?" I didn't even want to look at the remaining balance. I just hoped I had enough in there to buy food.

"I'd be happier if you stayed away from me."

I chewed another mouthful of toast, glaring back at him. "With pleasure. Stay away from me too."

"With pleasure," he mimicked with a curl of his lip.

Fuck him. Finishing up my toast as quickly as I could, I stood, gripping my mug of coffee. Anywhere was better than sitting in the kitchen with the guy who seemed determined to punish me for one mistake that, in my opinion, was just as much his fault as mine. "Thanks for the bread and milk, by the way."

Then I got out of there as quickly as I could before he registered what I was saying.

BECCA STEELE

The small supermarket close to the Mansions seemed to be full of students, all with the same idea as me. Picking up a basket, I grabbed the basics—bread, ramen noodles, pasta, and some cheap jars of pasta sauce. I added eggs, cheese, and bacon and a couple of other bits before the barcode scanner told me I'd hit my money limit.

I joined the queue for the self-service checkout. Too busy checking out my phone, I missed the line of people moving forwards until someone bumped into my back with a muttered apology.

"Shit, sorry." I turned around. "My fault. I wasn't paying attention."

The guy who'd bumped into me gave me an easy grin. "No problem." He cocked his head, his wavy, light brown hair falling across his eyes. "Wait, I know you. You were at the student union last night, but you left before I could introduce myself. You live at number 3, right?"

"Yeah." I glanced towards at the front of the queue and shuffled forwards before I turned back to him. "I'm Noah."

"Elliot. I live at number 1."

I smiled. "Hi. I've met two of your housemates already. Ander and Levi."

We both moved to checkouts next to each other and began to scan our items. He shot me a sideways glance. "You met the two footballers, then. I take it you're a footballer too?"

I shook my head, too violently, given the sudden humour in his eyes. "Nope. Definitely not. There was a mix-up with the housing, apparently. Levi was supposed to be moving into my house, and I was supposed to be in your house."

Elliot paused in scanning his items, letting his gaze rake over me. "Hmm. Shame."

Was he...fuck. If I had a gaydar, it was broken. I couldn't tell if I was imagining his interest in me.

"You've met three of us now, then." He was still studying me intently, and I could feel my cheeks flushing. Unbidden, an image of Liam flashed up in my mind. I pushed it away. Liam didn't deserve a second of my time, and even if he had a total personality transplant, it didn't change the fact that he was straight. "Why don't you come over sometime? You can meet my other housemates, JJ and Charlie, and we could have a beer or something?"

I cleared my suddenly dry throat. Fishing my debit card from my pocket, I held it over the card reader and held my breath until it beeped to say the payment had been successful. When I picked up my bags of food, relief coursing through me, I realised that Elliot was still standing there, waiting for a reply. "Yeah, okay. Sounds good."

"Looking forward to it."

"Uh. Yeah. Me too." A thought suddenly occurred to me. "Hey. Do you know where the closest gym is? Preferably one that's cheap."

He thought for a minute. "The uni has a gym, or there's a boxing gym nearby if you want something a bit quieter. Are you planning on joining any of the sports clubs? They subsidise your membership."

"No. Me and sports don't mix. I work out, and I run. But other sports are a no for me."

"You're in luck." He shot me another easy grin. "I'm in the running club. Want me to get you the details?"

"Yeah, that would be great, thanks."

Shifting his bags to one hand, he pulled out his phone.

"Here. Put your number in my contacts, and I'll send you all the info."

When we were done, I headed out of the shop with a smile on my face. Things were looking up.

SIX

NOAH

D amon glanced over at me as he passed me a joint. "Ready for lectures to start next week?"

The night breeze from the open lounge windows danced across my skin as I inhaled, smoke curling through the air, before handing it back to him. "Yeah, I think so. I've got all the books, at least."

"If either of you want any help, just shout. We're all studying business here, except for Travis," Preston cut in. "So one of us should have the answers if there's anything you need to know."

"Cheers. Appreciate it." Damon glanced up at him before inhaling the joint and collapsing back on the sofa.

Liam appeared in the doorway, a can of beer in hand, his hair all dishevelled and falling into his eyes. I bit the inside of my cheek, trying hard not to notice how good he looked.

He didn't even spare me a glance as he took the space farthest from me on the sofa. Not bothering with a greeting, he held out his hand to Damon. "Pass me that."

Everyone exchanged glances, and Travis cleared his throat. "Alright, Liam?"

Liam just lifted his hand in acknowledgement, exhaling a long curl of smoke from his mouth, and Travis rolled his eyes before giving Preston a pointed look. He nodded, taking the hint and changing the subject.

"Hey. Damon, Noah, there's a house party next door on Friday night if you guys want to go. Ander said it's open house, so if either of you want to bring anyone, feel free." He turned to me. "That reminds me—we need to set up a date for Revolve."

"Revolve?"

"The gay club." A grin curved over his lips. "I still need your help persuading Kian."

I returned his grin. "Yeah, I can do that. I need to wait until my student loan gets paid, though."

His smile dimmed. Leaning forwards, he studied me with concern. "Hey, man, I can lend you some money if you need it for anything. No questions asked."

"Uh. Thanks for the offer." It was so fucking awkward being in this situation. "I think I'll be okay. I've just got to stay away from anything that costs me money for a bit. I should have the loan next week, and I'm looking at applying for a couple of jobs."

"You really weren't lying when you said you didn't have any money?" Liam's voice broke the sudden silence, and my eyes flew to his. He looked almost...guilty? Chewing on his lip, he fidgeted in his seat.

I couldn't help my eye-roll. "Well, yeah. I don't make up that kind of shit for fun."

"Have I missed something?" Preston stared between us.

"No," we both answered at the same time, and he held up his hands.

"Okay. I think that's my cue to leave." He climbed to his feet and addressed the room in general. "Do *not* disturb me."

Travis pulled a face. "Keep it down if you're going to be having phone sex again."

Pausing in the doorway, Preston shot him an amused look. "Wear earplugs."

He shook his head. "I'll bear that in mind." Climbing to his feet, he stretched. "Actually, now you mention it, I'm taking that as my cue to leave too. I'll be at number 5 with Kira—"

"I'm coming." Damon immediately jumped to his feet, grinning at Travis' amused chuckle. His gaze flicked to Liam. "Liam? You coming?"

There was silence for a minute, and then Liam slowly shook his head. "Nah, I don't think so. Not this time. I'm gonna finish this up—" He held up the remains of the joint. "—then I've got shit to do."

"See ya later then." Damon saluted him, then disappeared out of the door with Travis. After a couple of minutes, I heard the front door close and then Preston's footsteps heading up the stairs. Liam remained locked in position, his eyes darting around the room, landing everywhere but on me.

Finally, I couldn't take it anymore. "I could've banged out the dent in your car, you know. Or you could've waited until my loan came in. Then you wouldn't have to feel bad."

The guilty expression immediately disappeared from his face, and his eyes flashed with anger as he glared at me. "Do you have to be such a fucking dick? And you fucking owe me bread and milk."

"Fine." Downing the rest of my beer in one go, I crushed the can in my hand, threw it onto the coffee table, and then stormed into the kitchen. At this point, I didn't even know why I was acting this way. Wasn't weed supposed to mellow you? I was the very fucking opposite of mellow.

Liam was right on my heels as I wrenched open the door to my food cupboard, pulling out my one and only loaf of bread. I ripped open the bag, grabbed two slices, and launched them at him. One of the slices completely missed him, dropping to the floor, but the other was a direct hit, smacking him right in the side of the face.

Shit.

We both froze, staring at each other. Then he lunged for me, and suddenly, his body was pinning me against the counter.

I couldn't breathe. He was so close. And so hot.

The next second, he was snarling in my face, his enraged breaths hitting my lips. "You're completely fucking crazy. Who the fuck throws *bread* at someone?"

His angry words cut the spell I was under, and an involuntary laugh burst out of me. Maybe he was right. Maybe I was crazy. Or maybe it was just the way he got under my skin that made me act this way. Whatever, it was kind of funny now I thought about it. I gripped the counter, trying to compose myself. It was a lost cause when I saw his lips twitch, and I knew he was holding back his own smile. Then I couldn't hold back my laughter.

"You're fucking crazy," he repeated, this time with far less heat. The corners of his lips kicked up the tiniest bit, and it made me feel warm inside.

Now we were so close together, I found myself noticing little details about him that I hadn't picked up on before, like the thickness of his lashes and the faint dusting of freckles across his nose.

He was *so* gorgeous.

My laughter died away, and I took an unsteady breath. "I'm sorry. I...I wasn't thinking straight. I didn't mean to do that." Without any conscious thought, I reached up to his cheek. "You've got breadcrumbs here." The second the pad of my finger made contact with his warm skin, he shivered.

His eyes widened, and he jumped back from me as if I'd burned him. Spinning on his heel, he shot out of the room and thundered up the stairs, leaving me standing in the kitchen with two wasted slices of bread at my feet, wondering what the fuck had possessed me to act the way I just had.

SEVEN

LIAM

Music pounded in my ears, and the crush of bodies made it impossible to spot my friends. As I pushed my way through, a girl stumbled into me, knocking my arm that held my beer, sending it splashing over both of us. I steadied her with a hand on her back as she gave me an apologetic smile.

"Sorry. I didn't see you there." Her smile turned flirtatious, her heated gaze running over me, and normally I'd be into it...but for some reason, I wasn't feeling it today.

"No worries. Excuse me." Spinning away from her, I continued on my way, heading in the direction of the door.

"Liam!"

I turned to see Ander making his way over to me, the crowds parting for him as usual.

"Alright?" I gave him a fist bump. "Nice party."

"Yeah." He flashed me a grin, then leaned closer. "All the girls from number 5 are here. That includes the new *single* girls. Want an intro?"

"I'm capable of pulling on my own, but thanks for the offer."

"You don't wanna work together? You know we make a good team." A mock pout appeared on his face, making me laugh.

"Fuck, yeah, we do, but I'm not in the mood for it yet. Need another drink first." I held up my bottle, and he nodded, accepting my excuse.

"That means I get first pick. Catch up with you later, mate."

When he'd disappeared, I downed the rest of my beer. There was a weird restless feeling inside me. I couldn't put my finger on what it was, but I didn't like it.

Only one thing for it.

More drinks.

———

Fuck, I was definitely wasted. Exiting the bathroom, I attempted to walk in a straight line, but when I stumbled into the wall, I decided fresh air was the answer.

What I didn't expect was to round the corner of the corridor and see my housemate with his tongue down another guy's throat. Yeah, he'd told us he was gay, and he'd even said something to me directly about being into dick, but saying it was one thing and actually seeing it in front of me was another.

I stopped dead, frozen in place, unable to drag my gaze away. I'd seen guys kissing before—my housemate, Preston, with his boyfriend, Kian, for one—so I didn't know why this was such a shock to the system. What the fuck was it about Noah that had me reacting so strongly all the time?

The guy had Noah pushed up against the wall, and he had one arm planted on the wall and the other around the back of Noah's neck, while Noah gripped his waist. As I watched, the guy's head moved down to Noah's throat.

That was when Noah's eyes met mine, and all that fucking heat was suddenly directed straight at me.

My mouth went dry.

He disentangled himself from the guy, all the while keeping his eyes on me. What the fuck was going on? His hand went down to the noticeable bulge in his jeans, and I swallowed hard as my dick jerked, completely out of the blue. My heart was pounding out of my chest, and my head was spinning, a weird buzz running through my body. Was I having some kind of panic attack?

Someone knocked into me, and I managed to break away from Noah's intense stare, spinning around and moving in the opposite direction as fast as I could. Suddenly, going outside to sober up sounded like the worst idea. I needed to wipe whatever that was from my mind.

Stumbling into the kitchen where all the drinks were, I dug around in the fridge for something stronger than beer.

"Liam."

I glanced up to see Travis with his arm slung around Kira's shoulders, holding up a bottle of bright green liquid. *Absinthe.* Lurching upright, I made my way over to them and took the bottle from his hand.

"You read my mind." Tipping it to my lips, I relished the liquorice burn of the alcohol sliding down my throat for about five seconds until I started coughing.

"Whoa. Careful there, mate," Travis cautioned me. "That's strong shit."

After a second, much smaller swig, I handed the bottle back to him, already feeling better. "Cheers. You guys having a good time?"

Travis glanced down at Kira with a smile before turning back to me. "First party of the year, innit? It's always good. Better their house than ours, though. This way, we don't have to deal with the clean-up." He peered at me closely. "Are you alright?"

I cleared my throat. "Yeah. Why wouldn't I be?"

Kira interrupted him before he could question me further, tilting her head to the side, tendrils of her wavy blonde hair swinging around her face. "Trav. Do you want to go back to yours in a bit? I think I'm almost at my limit of socialising tonight."

Unprompted, images flipped through my mind... A dark hallway...bodies pressed together...huge eyes with darkened pupils meeting mine...

I needed to get out of here too. Attempting a casual slouch against the wall, I gave them a nod. "I'll head back with you guys."

"We need to find Noah before we leave. Have you seen him? Travis wanted to keep an eye on him and Damon, what with it being their first student house party and all. You know he doesn't have his reputation as the dad of your house for nothing." Kira gave Travis an affectionate smile before scanning the crowds. "Damon's over there, but I haven't seen Noah all night."

My whole body tensed up at the mention of his name. Grabbing the bottle back from Travis, I took another swallow, wincing at the taste. "I think he's busy."

Travis gave me a weird look but didn't comment. I tipped back the bottle again, vaguely aware of Kira replying to me.

"Okay. Wait here if you want to come back with us. We're going to find Noah."

Time passed in a blur as I placed the bottle to my lips

yet again. When my vision started going hazy, I found myself leaning against a wall, then sliding down to the floor.

I closed my eyes.

"I've got him." Strong arms helped me stagger to my feet.

A groan came from my throat. "Make it stop spinning," I mumbled.

An amused chuckle sounded close to my ear as I was tugged along, leaning my body into the person holding me up. "Just hold on to me, yeah?"

Through my drunken haze, his words penetrated my consciousness.

Wait a fucking minute. I recognised that voice.

Peeling one of my eyelids back, I chanced a look at the person who was basically taking 90 percent of my body weight at this point. Amber eyes lit with amusement met mine. "Don't throw up on me," he warned.

I groaned again, slamming my eye shut. This had to be some kind of drunk hallucination. Fuck the fucking absinthe. I was never drinking again.

The next minute, there was a cool night breeze on my face, and then it stopped. The sound of a door slamming shut reverberated painfully through my skull. Low voices sounded close to me, but by then, I was already on my way to oblivion.

When I next peeled my eyes open, it took me a minute to get my bearings. My head felt like it was being attacked by a hammer, and my mouth was so dry that I couldn't even clear my throat without a painful scratching feeling.

"Liam?"

No. That couldn't be him. Not here, in my bedroom. My sacred space.

"What are you doing here?" I said hoarsely, letting my eyes shut again.

"Making sure you don't choke to death on your own puke. There's tablets and water on the side—you should probably have them now."

"I'm fine. You can leave."

"Yeah, you really look fine." I heard him moving, and then the side of the bed sank under his weight. "You threw up three times."

I had? I didn't remember that. My humiliation was now complete, and Noah needed to fucking leave. It was bad enough that he'd seen me like this, but being in my bedroom, watching me like some kind of nursemaid? "Get out."

"I don't want to lea—"

"Get. Out." My voice cracked, my raw throat making it hurt to speak. "*Please.*"

He sighed. "Fine. I'll leave. But you need to have these painkillers first."

Somehow, I managed to push myself up into a seated position, slumped against the headboard of my bed. With the room spinning around me, I watched, bleary-eyed, as Noah popped two painkillers out of the blister pack and handed them to me with the water. Knowing that it would be the quickest way to get him out of my room, I swallowed them without argument, letting the cool water soothe my mouth and throat. When I was done, I slid back down, my head still hammering. "Now leave."

His weight disappeared from the mattress, and finally, I heard the sound of my door closing.

Burying my face in my pillow with a groan, I succumbed to the blissful oblivion of sleep.

EIGHT

NOAH

"Morning." I made a show of looking at my watch when Liam appeared in the lounge, clasping a large mug in his hands, somehow still managing to look hot despite the fact that he was clearly hungover as fuck. "Or should I say afternoon?"

"Fuck off." He didn't even spare me a glance, dropping to the sofa next to Damon, who was engrossed in something on his laptop, his fingers tapping along with whatever he was listening to through his AirPods. When I glanced over at Liam, his cheeks were flushed, and his grip on his mug was so tight, his knuckles were white.

Right. No reminders of last night. I got the hint that he was hoping we'd both forget about it.

It wasn't that easy, though.

Last night...it had been a mistake to kiss that guy. I'd told myself that it was what I needed. This was part of what I'd been hoping my uni experience would be like—to be able to meet guys who were interested in me and to be out in the open with them. Not only that, but my enemy-slash-housemate had been occupying way too much of my head-space, and it had to stop.

But as soon as the guy had started to kiss me, it was clear that something was missing.

I'd tried to get into the kiss, but when he'd moved his mouth to my neck, I realised that it wasn't what I wanted. *He* wasn't what I wanted. I'd been set to break away from him when I'd noticed someone watching us.

Liam. He was half hidden in the shadows, his heavy-lidded gaze focused on me, and his mouth open as he stared at us. He swiped his tongue across his lips in a completely unconscious movement, and that was when my dick had gone from barely interested to extremely interested. I didn't know what had possessed me, but I'd moved away from the guy and palmed my cock through my jeans as Liam watched me, completely unmoving. I couldn't make out his expression, but he looked so fucking hot right then.

I'd *never* had that kind of reaction to someone before. Yeah, I'd noticed how hot Liam was from the moment I'd first seen him, but right then, it was like someone had turned the dial all the way up, and everything had been amplified to the point where I couldn't concentrate on anything else other than him.

He'd disappeared before I'd even had a chance to move. By the time I'd found him again, he was more or less passed out on the floor. A weird protective instinct had burned through me, seeing him like that, and I'd helped him out of the house. He'd passed out on my shoulder almost as soon as we'd got back inside number 3, and Travis and I had to prac-tically carry him up the stairs. I'd managed to get him into the bathroom just in time before he'd been sick three times in a row, and then I'd just about managed to manhandle him onto his bed where he'd fallen asleep. I hadn't dared to leave him in case he was sick again. I'd only taken enough time to find water and painkillers, and then I'd curled up on his small sofa and dozed for a few hours before he'd woken up and kicked me out of his room. That had kind of hurt, although it shouldn't have. I hadn't been expecting a thanks, given that we were barely on speaking terms.

Now, I took the chance to study him while he stared at the TV, drinking his coffee. I dropped the teasing because he really didn't look good.

"How are you feeling?" I said softly.

"Why do you care?" he snapped. "It's just a hangover."

"Okay. Just a question." I attempted to keep my voice calm, even though my natural instinct was to answer back. When he turned to glare at me, I stood abruptly and walked out of the lounge. There was no way I could stay in the same room as him anymore and not get into an argument, and I'd only end up feeling guilty if I antagonised him while he was in this state.

I ran into Travis in the hallway, entering the other downstairs room with all his media equipment.

"Noah! Just the man I was looking for. You got a minute?"

"I'm free. What do you need?"

He beckoned me into the room, where Kira was winding up a black electrical cable. "Babe. I found us a cameraman."

A bright smile spread across her face. "Perfect. Shall we set up in the kitchen? Noah, can you grab that ring light, please?"

"This better not be a porno or anything. What am I supposed to be doing?" I asked as I lugged a light and some kind of reflector thing into the kitchen.

Travis set a small case on the kitchen table and

unzipped it, handing me a camera. "No porn involved, so you can get your mind out of the gutter. It's a project for one of my modules. We're going to be baking, and you're going to film us."

I had so many questions, but the first one out of my mouth was, "Can you bake?"

They both laughed at that, shaking their heads. "Nope, but it's for my project. I have to upload it to my YouTube channel and analyse—never mind. Point is, I have to do it, and it's probably gonna be a disaster," Travis said. With an amused chuckle, I leaned back against the counter with the camera in my hands, waiting for further instructions.

Once they had everything set up, Travis showed me how to work the camera and then showed me a couple of video clips to give me an idea of the filming style he wanted. He waved away my concerns about having never filmed anyone before. "You'll be fine. Just keep the camera on us, zoom in whenever you think we need a close-up, and don't let it shake. You can't go wrong."

By the time the two of them were piping the batter into their cake cases, the kitchen was a disaster zone. As Kira was flicking batter from the spoon at Travis, Liam walked in. He frowned at me as I placed a finger to my lips, then raised a brow as he took in the state of Travis and Kira. Avoiding the camera, he picked his way through the unidentified ingredients that had ended up all over the floor and came up to my side.

My whole body hummed with awareness as he leaned into my personal space, his breath hitting my ear. "How much longer is this shit going on for? I'm hungover as fuck, and I need food," he whispered in a low rasp.

Carefully holding the camera steady with one hand, I

held up my other hand, splaying my fingers. *Five minutes*, I mouthed.

He huffed and stepped away, and the tension drained from my body.

As soon as the cakes were in the oven, I placed the camera down and turned to face him. He was pale beneath his tan, and there were dark circles under his eyes. I couldn't help the wave of sympathy that went through me, even though his pain was self-inflicted.

For some reason, I wanted to take care of him. "I guess I owe you some bread. Want some toast?"

Surprise crossed his features, but then he nodded, biting his lip. I headed over to my cupboard and pulled out what remained of my loaf of bread. As I popped two slices in the toaster, I felt his gaze on me. At this point, though, I knew better than to catch his eye. I'd only be rewarded with a cutting look or comment. So instead, I busied myself with grabbing a plate and butter.

His gaze still burned into me, hot and heavy.

"Just butter? Marmite? Nutella?" I chanced a look at him once I'd examined the contents of his cupboard. He was quiet for a change, still watching me but rubbing his temples, his forehead creased.

"I can do it." His frown deepened. "I'm hungover, not sick."

"It's okay. I owe you."

"That's true," he muttered. "Marmite, then." Pushing away from the counter, he took a seat at the kitchen table, burying his head in his arms on the table with a groan.

"Bit hungover, mate?" Travis smirked, receiving an elbow in the ribs from a laughing Kira. "Regretting *la fée verte*?" Liam didn't bother lifting his head, but he moved his hand so he could give Travis the middle finger.

Shaking my head, I turned away from them, flicking the switch on the kettle. Once the toast was done and I'd made coffees for everyone, I handed mugs to Travis and Kira, then carried Liam's coffee and toast over to the table.

"Toast's ready." When Liam didn't respond, I sighed. I prodded him on the shoulder...or I meant to, but it somehow turned into more of a caress, my finger trailing across the top of his arm. I heard him breathe in sharply, his body stiffening in surprise, and I quickly yanked my hand away. What the fuck was I doing?

Luckily Travis and Kira hadn't noticed anything, too busy getting ready to film the rest of the segment. I took my position behind the camera again, glad that I had it to hide behind. I didn't dare to look over at Liam.

I managed to successfully ignore him as I zoomed in on what was supposed to be cakes, if you could call the flat, collapsed discs of sponge "cakes." By the time Travis and Kira were flinging icing at each other instead of decorating the cakes, Liam was finished with his toast and heading in the direction of the door.

Halfway across the kitchen, he paused, then took a detour.

"Thanks for the toast," he murmured as he brushed past me. His cheeks were a little flushed, and he wouldn't look at me, but just that tiny bit of contact set off a chain reaction of goosebumps across my body.

Then he was gone, and I was helpless to stop the tiny smile that tugged at the corners of my lips.

NINE

NOAH

"I'm sorry, but there's nothing I can do. The form was completed incorrectly." The woman behind the counter in the student finance office swivelled her monitor around to show me. "There should have been an additional zero there, and you should have ticked this box. Oh, and we need an email address and phone number for the supervisor at your father's previous place of employment," she informed me in a bored tone.

"What am I supposed to do? My account is empty. How am I supposed to eat?" I rubbed my hand across my face. How could this be fucking happening?

She stared at me, completely unsympathetic. "You'll have to wait until the amended form goes through the system. Once it's gone through and been approved, the loan will be paid into your account within five working days."

How had everything gone wrong so quickly? Two months ago, I wouldn't have even needed student loans. But then my dad had been made redundant from his job as an AI engineer, and so far, he was having trouble finding anything else. There was also the fact that a big chunk of my parents' savings had gone on paying for my grandparents' retirement home, and my sisters needed providing for. Money was tight now.

As I stalked down the road towards the house, anger burned through me. Mostly at myself, but partly at Liam. If only he'd been more reasonable, I could've easily knocked out the dent in his car or waited a bit longer to pay him the money. Literally anything was better than this. Nothing left in my bank account, down to the last of my food, and no guarantee when I'd have any more.

Inside the house, I went straight to the kitchen. As I thought. I had enough food left for two, maybe three meals if I was lucky. Fuck. What was I supposed to do? I guess if it came to it, I'd have to swallow my pride and ask if anyone minded loaning me some money. The problem, other than my pride, was that I didn't know exactly when I'd be able to pay them back.

My anger disappeared, and now I just felt miserable. I trudged up the stairs to my bedroom, not wanting to be around anyone else right now. Throwing myself onto my bed, I blinked back the unexpected tears that were threatening. How was I such a fuckup already when I'd barely begun university? LSU was supposed to be my fresh start, and I'd been determined to make it work, even though I'd be relying on the money from my student loan, whenever it finally came in, because I wasn't going to let my parents dig into their savings for me. I'd seen this as my chance to prove to them, and to myself, that I could stand on my own two feet. But I was already failing.

My phone rang, disturbing me from my depressing thoughts.

Mum.

"Hi, Mum." Thankfully, my voice sounded more or less normal.

"Noah."

A wave of sudden homesickness hit me as her warm voice came through the speaker, accompanied by the background noise of Layla's and Ami's high-pitched voices.

"I wanted to see how you were getting on." Worry threaded through her tone. "Did your student loan come through?"

"Yeah, all fine," I said, lying through my teeth. I bit the inside of my cheek as I heard a palpable sigh of relief through the speaker.

"Thank goodness. There's some good news on the horizon, or so I hope." There was a pause where she told my sisters to quieten down, and then she returned her attention to me. "Dad's got a job interview next Wednesday, so keep your fingers crossed for him."

A cautious hope filled me. "That's great. What's the job?"

She gave me a quick rundown of the position, which, from what I could tell, sounded similar to his previous job. That had to be a good sign, surely. Before I had a chance to ask any questions, my sisters were wrestling the phone from her, and then they were both trying to talk to me at once. My mood lifted instantly. I spent the next ten minutes listening to their breathless rambling as they both raced to tell me all their news, talking over the top of each other. Eventually, my mum was back on the other end of the phone. "Keep everything crossed. Dad's..." Her voice cracked, and she sniffed. It was like a punch to the gut, hearing her upset. "The redundancy hit him hard. He feels like he's let us all down. You, especially."

My stomach churned. "What? He hasn't let me down. This wasn't his fault at all."

"I'm sorry, I shouldn't have said anything. I don't want to put this on you. You should be enjoying your time, not worrying about anything." Clearing her throat, she attempted a cheerful tone. "At least I can tell Dad that your loan came through so he can stop worrying about that. He's been so concerned, Noah. I'm almost glad you weren't here to see...never mind. I hope you know that as soon as he gets another job, everything will be back to normal."

"I wish there was something I could do. I know you refused to let me before, but you know I can defer a year, and get a job instead. I want to help."

My mum pointedly cleared her throat, and I could picture the severe look coming over her face, that stubborn set to her mouth that meant whatever anyone said, she'd made her mind up and wouldn't be swayed. "Absolutely not. You carry on as you are. Enjoy yourself. Make the most of student life. We're okay, Noah. We're not living on the breadline by any means. We just have to make some adjustments."

"Just say the word if you need me. I—"

"We're not discussing this any further. Now, tell me. Have you met any nice boys?"

"Mum," I groaned. "I'm *not* talking about this with you. Ask me anything else."

She laughed at that. "Okay. Tell me how your classes are going."

I spent another fifteen minutes or so talking to her before she had to go to prepare dinner. After placing my phone next to my bed, I fell back onto my duvet, and closed my eyes.

The next thing I knew, there was a pounding at my

door. Blinking, I dragged myself up into a seated position, glancing at my phone. Guess I'd fallen asleep because it was now almost 9:00 p.m. "Yeah?" I called.

Travis' voice sounded through the door. "There's two-for-one drinks at the student union tonight. Are you coming?"

"Not tonight, mate. Thanks for the invite, though."

"Okay. If you change your mind, we'll probably be there most of the night."

"Will do. Have fun."

A little while later, I headed into the bathroom to splash some water on my face, grimacing at the redness around my eyes. Then, I made my way downstairs.

The house was silent, empty. In the kitchen, I spooned yesterday's leftover pasta into a bowl and dumped it in the microwave to warm through.

If I'd known what was coming, I would've just eaten it cold.

There was a loud crack, and everything went off. The microwave, the fridge, the lights...everything.

"Fuck!" I shouted. Fumbling for my phone, I hit the button to turn the torch on, then uselessly pressed the kitchen light switch a few times in case it magically decided to work again. What was I supposed to do?

I sent a text to Travis.

Me: Are you home? Power went off

He replied almost instantly, to my relief.

Travis: Not home but power is dodgy sometimes. Flip the trip switches on the circuit breaker and it'll come back on

Me: Where's that?

After waiting for a few minutes with no reply, I decided to go on a hunt. I could deal with this. I hadn't actually touched a circuit breaker before, but I had Google. I knew the one at my parents' house was in the cupboard under the stairs, so I turned on my phone torch and made my way into the hallway, holding my phone up in front of me.

I crashed straight into Liam. He was moving so fast, and I was so unprepared, I staggered back, losing my balance and smacking into the wall behind me. My head hit the plaster with a painful thump, and my phone dropped to the floor. We were suddenly surrounded by darkness.

"Watch where you're fucking going," I hissed, my earlier anger towards him coming back in a rush.

"Same to you," he snapped. I could barely make him out in the dark hallway.

"Wanker," I muttered.

"What did you call me?" He was suddenly up in front of me, all tense and riled up. It was too much to deal with. I shoved against him, moving out of his space. My hand went to the back of my head, and I stifled a pained groan as I felt the sore spot that was already forming there.

Instead of replying to his question and getting into yet another argument, I concentrated on the task at hand. "Do you know where the circuit breaker is?"

"Yes."

It sounded like he was speaking through gritted teeth. His breath was coming in short gasps, and I'd bet anything he was right on the edge of completely losing his temper, if our previous encounters were anything to go by.

"Do you know what to do?"

"Yes," he said again, and this time, his voice was much

closer. I raised my hand, and it landed on solid muscle. His chest? I left it there for a heartbeat, hearing his sharp intake of breath. *What the fuck am I doing?* I yanked it away.

"Can you—" I licked my lips. "Can you show me what to do? Please?"

"I suppose so." His voice had a huskiness that wasn't normally there, and it sent heat curling through me. Doing my best to ignore it, I carefully felt around on the floor with my foot until it hit the edge of my phone, then swiped it from the floor. The tiny beam of light from the torch was welcome, but I kept it pointed down so it didn't blind us. And maybe I didn't want to see Liam's face either.

He fished his own phone out of his pocket and turned on his torch, and I followed him, not towards the understairs cupboard, where I'd been heading, but into the room that Travis had all his media stuff in. Mounted on the wall, next to the door, there was a large box I hadn't noticed.

"This switch is for the lighting circuit." Liam shone his torch at the row of switches, focusing on the one on the far right. I stepped closer to him so I could see better. He angled the beam. "There's the downstairs electric, and the upstairs is on that one."

"What do we do?"

For some reason, both of us were speaking in whispers. Maybe it was because we were in the dark and the house was so silent. Without realising it, I'd stepped so close to him that our shoulders were brushing against each other's.

"Noah."

"Yeah?" I turned my head, catching the glint of his blue eyes in the light of my torch as he also turned. For a minute, we both stood there, our eyes locked, the press of his arm against mine more insistent.

"I—" He cut himself off, swallowing hard. "Sorry for making you bang your head."

I was suddenly completely aware of our proximity and the fact that we were completely alone in the house. "It's... it's okay. Sorry for snapping at you." My voice came out way too hoarse.

He swallowed again, the sound loud in the silence. "Who was that guy you were kissing at the party?"

My mouth fell open. Of all the questions he could ask me, this was the last thing I expected. "Ander's party? That...that was no one. I didn't even get his name."

"*Oh.*" He breathed the word, and I felt the soft huff of his breath on my lips.

Unconsciously, I leaned even closer to him, so close that I clearly heard his shaky exhale. I slid my tongue across my lips, and his eyes grew wide and dark.

"Liam," I whispered.

I caught the panic flitting across his face as he spun away from me so fast, I wouldn't have been surprised if he'd got whiplash. He reached up to the switches quickly, flipping them one by one. The power and lights came back on in a rush, and he practically ran to get away from me.

Maybe it was my imagination, but for a moment there... no. I wasn't going to let myself think about what might have been.

Except that was a lie. Later that night, in the privacy of my bedroom, I curled my hand around my hard dick. My eyes fell shut, and although I tried to steer my thoughts in a different direction, it was all too easy to remember the way he'd rasped out my name. It had been so fucking hot, and my imagination easily supplied the image of him saying my name and then dropping to his knees and taking me in his mouth.

My hand moved faster.

Dirty, dirty thoughts of my housemate filled my mind, until I came, hard, covering my hand and my abs with my release.

When I caught my breath, I groaned into my pillow.

I was *so* fucked. And not in a good way.

TEN

LIAM

After that weird-as-fuck moment with Noah when the power went out, I tried, and mostly succeeded, to avoid him over the next few days. Something about him rubbed me up the wrong way. I couldn't put my finger on it, but he affected me in a way I hadn't experienced with anyone else before. It wasn't ideal when we were house-mates, but the house was big, and all of us were busy now that the semester had started.

Measuring out my pasta with my AirPods in, I was zoned out and lost in my own world when Preston's voice sounded loudly next to me, making me jump. "Noah! Have you eaten yet?" He turned to me with a grin, speaking at a normal volume. "Didn't see me there, huh?"

I rolled my eyes at him just as Noah's reply came faintly from the lounge.

"I'll grab something later."

A frown appeared on Preston's face, and I paused my music, my brows pulling together. "What's wrong? What's that look for?"

He glanced at the doorway before lowering his voice as

he spooned noodles between two bowls. "Didn't you hear about Noah's student loan being delayed? I offered to help him out, but he turned me down. I'm betting he's too proud to ask for help, but you only have to look at the state of his food cupboard to see he's struggling."

Fuck.

Guilt hit me like a sledgehammer.

Preston disappeared out of the door, bowl in hand, and I returned to prepping my food. I stared at the saucepan in front of me for a long moment, my jaw clenched tight enough to give me the beginnings of a headache, before I tipped up the bag and added double my usual amount of pasta.

When the pasta was done, I stirred in pesto from a jar, which was about as far as my cooking skills stretched. Then I headed into the lounge.

Preston didn't glance up from where he was shovelling noodles into his mouth while watching the TV with Kian, who was staying over for the weekend. Someone else noticed me, though. Noah raised his head, his eyes flicking to mine for the barest second before his jaw tightened and he returned his gaze to the TV.

"Uh, Noah?" Folding my arms in front of me, I leaned back against the door frame.

"What?" He didn't bother looking at me again.

"You got a minute?"

There was a second where I wasn't sure if he was going to ignore me, but then he climbed to his feet with a sigh. He followed me into the kitchen, where he stopped in the doorway, refusing to meet my gaze. "What is it?"

"Can you sit down?"

"What is it?" he repeated. "I don't have time for this."

"Yeah, because you looked so busy watching the TV

back there," I muttered, causing him to glare at me. "Look, just sit down for a sec, okay?"

"Fine." He huffed loudly just to show how much of an annoyance it was, so I made sure he caught my eye-roll as he sat down.

"Wait there." Before he could say anything else, I headed over to the hob, splitting the pasta between two bowls, and then grabbed a couple of forks. Carrying the bowls over to the table, I placed one in front of him.

"Eat."

His eyes flew to mine, wide with shock. "What?"

"Eat," I repeated.

"I'm not a charity case." The tiny hitch in his voice was the only thing that stopped me from snapping at him as he pushed the bowl away from him, setting his jaw.

"Fuck, you're stubborn." I shoved the bowl back in his direction. "Ease my conscience, then."

"Why should I do you any favours?"

"*Please.*"

His shoulders slumped, and he picked up his fork.

We dug into the food in silence, and it was way too awkward, so I scrolled through my phone, hitting one of my Spotify playlists at random and linking it to the kitchen speaker.

Music blared through the kitchen, cutting straight through the strained atmosphere.

"Justin Bieber? Really?" He raised a brow. "Interesting choice."

Fuck. "No, wait, that's not mine." I stabbed at my phone screen so hard, I sent my phone skittering across the table.

"If you say so." A sudden grin appeared on his face, making me completely lose my train of thought. "I never would've taken you for a Belieber."

"Stop, please," I groaned, dropping my fork and burying my face in my arms. "I thought it was a different playlist."

"'Course you did. No need to be ashamed of it. This song's alright."

Raising my head, I attempted a glare, which was really fucking difficult when he was there grinning at me like the Cheshire cat. "I wouldn't be ashamed *if* it was my fucking playlist."

"Way too much protesting to be convincing. You should work on that." Shaking his head, he just kept on grinning.

I couldn't stop my lips from tugging up at the corners. "Irritating little shit, aren't you?"

"Little?" His jaw dropped, all mock indignation. "Fuck off. That extra inch you have on me is irrelevant."

He seemed to realise what he'd just said because his cheeks flushed, and he suddenly seemed very interested in the contents of his bowl. "I mean, uh, your height—"

I decided to take pity on him. "I know what you meant." Ducking my head to hide my smile, I turned back to my food. We were silent again while the music played softly in the background, but this time, it was easier.

When we'd both finished, he dropped his fork into his bowl with a clatter. "Liam?" When I raised my eyes to meet his, he looked at me almost hesitantly. "Thanks for the food."

"Yeah, well. I guess I should take some responsibility for all this."

Surprising me, he shook his head. "Nah. I mean, yeah, if you'd let me knock out the dent in the first place, I would've had my money. But I get it. It's your car. I don't get to decide how you fix it."

Did he want an apology? "I'm, uh, sorry?"

"No need to sound so sure about it."

"You *did* drive into me," I pointed out.

"Your fault too."

"See." I pointed my fork at him accusingly. "Irritating shit."

He stood, grinning, piling my bowl on top of his. "Just for that, since the dishwasher's full, you can do the washing up."

I stood, following him over to the sink. "Nope. I cooked. You have to wash up. Want a beer?"

"Yeah, okay." This time, he wasn't so hesitant about accepting something from me. "After I've washed this stuff."

The washing up didn't take long since we only had a few things. When he was putting the saucepan back in the cupboard, I grabbed a couple of beers from the fridge, then handed one to him.

"Does this mean things are okay between us?" he asked quietly as we headed back towards the lounge.

"Yeah."

One simple word, but the resulting expression on his face was so happy, it made me feel...fuck, I didn't know. *Good*. Glad we'd moved past the shit where we'd been on edge around each other.

Sprawled out on the lounge sofas, we were in the middle of a game with Preston and Kian when Noah's phone rang. He excused himself to answer it, disappearing out of the room.

"Sorted out your differences?" Preston side-eyed me, and I took his moment of distraction to shoot his character in the chest.

"That was a low blow," he muttered.

I smirked, keeping my eyes focused on the screen. "Should've been paying attention. But yeah, it's all good now. You noticed we had..."

"Issues? Yeah. You weren't subtle about it. But for what it's worth, I'm glad you've sorted them out now. Noah's a good guy." The End Game notification flashed up on the screen, and he stood, changing the subject, to my relief. "Anyone want another drink?"

When he'd disappeared from the room, I turned to Kian, needing to get the subject off my annoying house-mate. Literally *anything* would be better than talking about Noah. "How's things in Alstone?"

He shot me a quick grin. "Much better. I moved into an apartment next to the campus with Carter, did Preston say?"

I knew he'd had issues with his parents, so I wasn't surprised he'd left home. Carter was Kian's best friend, and his girlfriend, Raine, attended LSU. Carter and Kian both attended Alstone College, so it made sense that they'd moved in together. "No, he didn't say, but I'm happy for you, mate."

"Cheers. Should've done it sooner. Ever since Preston..." He trailed off, shaking his head. "Whatever. I'm glad to be out of there."

The question fell from my mouth without thought. "Your parents didn't take it well when you told them you were bi? Or was it Preston they had a problem with?"

"Yeah. It wasn't anything to do with Preston."

"Sorry." I shouldn't have even brought it up. He didn't owe me an explanation.

Slumping back on the sofa, he grunted, "Not like I expected anything else from them. Anyway, that's one of the many reasons I left. There was shit going on before I even came out to them."

"You... Sorry. Some people are bastards."

We lapsed into a bit of an awkward silence before Kian laughed. "Fuck this heavy shit. Play again?"

He restarted the game, and we both focused on the screen. But I couldn't stop the questions from surfacing. "Tell me to fuck off if you don't want to talk about it, but you're bi... What—how does it work for you?" Shaking my head, I groaned under my breath, attempting to gather my thoughts. "No, I don't mean that. I mean—have you always been into men and women?"

He hummed, taking a minute before he replied. And shooting my character in the head while he was at it too.

"Yeah. Before I got together with Preston, I'd only ever been with girls, but I'd been curious, I guess. I knew I found other guys hot. Just not enough to want to do anything about it until him."

I mashed the square button on the controller, slashing at his character on-screen, unsure how to reply. What the fuck had possessed me to even start asking him about it in the first place? It was none of my business.

"What about you?"

It took me a second to realise that Kian was asking me a question. "Me? Noooo. I'm straight. Women only."

From the corner of my eye, I saw his brows fly up, but then he schooled his expression.

"What's that face for? I'm not gonna be weird around you if that's what you're worried about."

"No." He shook his head. "I didn't think that. I've known you long enough to know you're cool."

"But—" I didn't get a chance to ask him anything else because Noah burst back into the room, Preston right behind him.

"My dad got the job!" He was practically vibrating with happiness and relief.

Kian stopped the game, switching back to the menu screen before standing up and crossing over to give him a brief, kind of awkward hug that mostly involved whacking him on the back. How had they managed to become so friendly when Noah had only lived here for about five minutes and Kian didn't even live here at all? How was it that Kian knew what was happening right now?

A weird feeling that felt disturbingly close to jealousy went through me.

"This calls for a celebratory beer or two. Preston? Wanna get Travis and your other housemate?" Kian grinned at Noah, and I clenched my teeth.

I remained seated. Noah and I definitely weren't at the hugging stage. Noah glanced over at me, clearly reading my mind because a cocky little smirk appeared on his face. He raised his brows, a challenge in his eyes. "Not gonna give me a congratulatory hug?"

"Fuck you. Fine." Dropping my controller on the coffee table, I jumped up, giving him the shortest hug possible.

That was the plan, anyway.

His arms came around me, and I couldn't help stiffening.

Why was he so fucking warm?

"Not a hugger, huh?" His amused laugh vibrated against my chest. That weird fucking feeling was back again, tugging at me.

"Not really." How could I explain that it had been a long, long time since anyone had hugged me properly? Celebratory hugs during football matches didn't count, and I tried to avoid anything couple-y like cuddling or holding hands with anyone I slept with.

He dropped his arms, immediately releasing me. "Sorry.

I didn't mean to make you feel uncomfortable. I was just teasing."

"It's okay."

Biting his lip, he lowered his gaze. "Yeah, but I—"

"Noah. Don't worry about it," I replied absentmindedly, my gaze caught on his mouth, his bottom lip shiny from where he'd been tugging it between his teeth. Why did he have to chew on it like that? Didn't he realise how distracting it was?

Taking a seat again, I moved on to safer subjects. He didn't need to know how I was too fucked up to hug him without having an internal crisis, and he definitely didn't need to notice me staring at his mouth like some kind of weirdo. "Your dad got a job?"

His face brightened, and he threw himself down next to me. "Yeah. It's a real weight off my mind."

As Preston returned to the room with Travis and Damon in tow, carrying a pack of beers, Noah told us about his dad's redundancy and how he'd been dealing with the burden of worrying about his family and struggling with his own subsequent money issues. The words tripped over themselves, the relief evident in his voice as he confided in us.

All the while, the guilt weighed on me, heavier and heavier. Why had I acted like such an asshole towards him? Why hadn't I stopped to consider that maybe he had a reason for his actions? Yeah, he'd been an asshole to me too, but that didn't excuse my behaviour.

Later, when everyone was talking amongst themselves, I leaned over to him. We'd somehow ended up sitting fairly close together on the sofa, so it was easy enough to lean in and speak without being overheard. "If I'd known, I wouldn't have asked for the money."

His reply was so soft that I strained to hear him. "I know." He pressed his thigh against mine, just the lightest touch, but my breath stuttered at the contact.

Out of the corner of my eye, I saw him smile, and something small and warm unfurled inside me.

ELEVEN

NOAH

Over the next couple of weeks, I managed to work out a routine that I was happy with. My student loan had come in, my dad had a confirmed start date for his new job, and now that I didn't have the money worries hanging over my head, I was free to concentrate on my coursework and uni life. I'd settled into my classes, and I had a weekly date with the running club. I normally tried to get in another run either on my own or with Elliot whenever I had a decent chunk of free time, and worked out in the uni gym as often as I could too. Exercise cleared my head, and although the professors were taking it easy on us in our first semester, I needed that mental break.

"Noah!"

I yanked my headphones off, hitting the button to slow the treadmill to a walking pace. Preston stood next to my treadmill with a grin on his face, with Travis and Liam on either side of him. "I just spoke to Kian. Do you still want to go to Revolve? I might have used you as a convenient excuse to persuade him to come with us. I said you needed the moral support."

It took me a minute to work out what he meant, and then I nodded. "Yeah. Definitely. When?"

"Friday?"

"Count me in, and feel free to use me as an excuse anytime."

"Revolve? My cousin works there. I can get him to give you a bit of a discount on drinks," Elliot interjected from the treadmill next to mine. "I can probably get you on the guest list too, if you want."

I glanced over at him. "Wanna come with us? Apparently, I need the moral support."

Both he and Preston laughed, and then he nodded. "Yeah, that would be great."

Liam's gaze bounced between Elliot and me, his eyes hard. I gritted my teeth, steeling myself. What was his problem now? I thought we were past all the hostility. It had seemed like we were on our way to becoming friends, in fact.

His words completely shocked me.

"I'll come."

Everyone turned to stare at him. Preston exchanged glances with Elliot before leaning closer to Liam and speaking in a low voice. "You know it's a gay club?"

Liam rolled his eyes at him. "Yeah, I'm aware of that. What, I'm not allowed to come because I'm straight?"

"No, I—"

"Okay, so I'll come. Trav? Spot me on the bench press?" Liam abruptly turned and began heading over to the free weights area of the gym. Travis looked at Preston and shrugged, before following Liam.

Liam had invited himself on our night out. Why?

When I'd finished my cool-down, I headed over to the weights area, and it was a complete coincidence that Liam still happened to be there, sitting back on one of the chest press machines, his muscles straining with the effort as he gripped the machine handles, moving them back and forth in a steady rhythm.

My stomach flipped, and I swallowed hard. He looked so good.

Fuck.

This was worse than I thought. Why did I have to become fixated on him, of all people? My stupid fucking brain, or more like my stupid fucking dick, was clearly broken. Nothing could ever happen with him.

Quickly, I moved to sit on the machine next to him, shoving the pin into the stack of weights at a level I was comfortable with. I'd been going for about eight reps when there was a clang next to me, and suddenly, Liam was standing in front of me with his brows pulled together.

"You're doing it wrong. You need to breathe properly. It'll make things easier."

"Huh?" I stared at him.

"You're holding your breath. You need to breathe in when you pull it towards you, then breathe out when you push against the weight." Huffing impatiently, he tapped the machine. "Move. I'll show you."

"Uh, okay." Was I about to pass up a chance to openly watch him work out? Not likely.

Taking my place on the machine, he pulled the pin out of the stack. "Start with no weight, get the technique right."

"I guess you're about to tell me I need to work on that too, huh?"

"Yep. Watch the master at work." He flashed a quick grin at my eye-roll before gripping the handles and moving the machine in a slow, precise way, inhaling and exhaling exaggeratedly. My eyes were drawn to his flexing muscles and the way his T-shirt clung to his skin, damp with sweat.

"See?"

"Yes," I croaked, my mouth dry. It was taking every ounce of my concentration to keep my dick in check. The way I reacted to him... The sooner I got over this, the better.

Oblivious to my drama, he hopped up from the machine, and then he was *right there*, all hot and sexy. "You try it."

Sinking onto the machine on shaky legs, I breathed in deeply, trying to get myself under control.

Iwillnothaveabonerinthegym, *Iwillnothaveaboner-inthegym.*

Then he pulled his shirt over his head, and *fuck me. Those abs.* I shifted on my seat, desperately casting around for anything unsexy for my brain to focus on, to stop what was about to become a very fucking obvious problem.

"Noah?"

"Huh." Great, I was reduced to monosyllables now.

"Focus. Breathe with me." When his hand unexpectedly slid onto my chest, I gasped out loud. There was no way he wouldn't be able to feel my heart racing under his palm. I watched as concern filled his eyes. "Your heart rate shouldn't be this elevated after just a few reps."

"It's. Not. The. Machine," I strangled out through gritted teeth. *Kill me now.*

"It's—*oh.*" His gaze darted down to my shorts, and he ripped his hand away from my chest, his eyes going wide and dark. "I think you've got it," he managed, then actually ran from me, dodging around the machines and disappearing through the doors that led to the changing rooms. I would have laughed if I hadn't been so mortified.

Collapsing forwards, I buried my face in my hands, groaning.

"That was awkward, wasn't it?" came the way-too-amused voice from my left.

"Please tell me you didn't witness the whole thing." I spoke into my hands, unwilling to face Travis, my cheeks hot and flaming.

"Let's see...you were staring at Liam like he was your favourite meal, then, yeah. I caught the rest."

"Please. Just kill me."

He laughed. When I finally risked raising my gaze to his, glaring at his amusement, his laughter finally died away. Lowering his voice, he took a step closer. "What I found interesting was Liam's reaction to you."

"What do you mean?" I asked, but he'd already turned his back to me and was sauntering away. I debated chasing after him, but I'd had just about enough humiliation for one day.

Fuck my life.

TWELVE

NOAH

I t was one of those evenings where the house was full, which made life easier. I wasn't going to hide away in my room. I'd spent most of the afternoon hiding in the library, where I'd made myself feel better by reading Reddit accounts of people getting boners at the most inconvenient of times. Mine paled in comparison to some of the stories.

Still, I had to live with Liam, and at the moment, my humiliation was fresh. So I was using the 'healthy' coping mechanism of drinking alcohol and engrossing myself in conversation with literally anyone and everyone that wasn't Liam. We'd all migrated to the kitchen somehow, and he'd ended up on the opposite side of the room to me, clearly feeling the same about needing space. It was probably more awkward for him than me. Probably.

Over at the kitchen table, Travis, Preston, and Damon were playing poker with a couple of the guys from next door. Liam was across the kitchen from me, leaning casually against the counter, deep in conversation with Ander and another guy who I vaguely recognised as being one of their football teammates. I stood against the opposite counter, half talking to Kira and one of her friends, picking at the label on my beer bottle, and stealing covert glances at Liam. Every time I thought about what had happened at the gym, I could feel my face heating, and I gulped down more alcohol in an effort to forget.

But I couldn't help looking. My eyes were drawn to him like magnets. Cliché as fuck, but true.

The third time I looked at him, he was watching me.

His cheeks flushed, and he snapped his gaze away instantly. I feigned a sudden interest in Kira's account of a former reality TV girl who had become a huge YouTuber, but it was almost a compulsion to glance back at Liam.

He was looking at me again.

But again, he immediately wrenched his gaze away from mine.

"Noah! Liam! Ander! Poker?"

Travis' shout cut through my whirling thoughts, and I spun towards the table to see that some of the poker players had disappeared, leaving just Travis and Preston. Gripping my beer, I made my way over to the table, sinking down onto the empty bench seat.

As soon as I sat down and Ander was sliding into the empty chair that we'd grabbed from the lounge earlier, I realised my mistake. There was only one spare seat, and it was on the bench next to me.

Fucking hell. Just when I was trying to avoid Liam.

I shifted as far over on the bench as I could, but I still felt his body heat when he sank down next to me. He seemed to be staying as far away from me as he could too, angling himself towards the edge of the table, but the gap between us was minimal. Bloody tiny benches.

Travis was quick to deal the cards, which was good

because it gave me something else to concentrate on. Something other than Liam's proximity.

I managed to dredge up a previously unknown talent for acting, throwing myself into the game and gambling my chips recklessly. We weren't playing for money, anyway, so it didn't really matter.

Sometime during the game, I realised that both Liam and I had moved closer together, and every time he moved his arm, the fabric of his hoodie brushed against my bare arm. Fuck my body for broadcasting how he was affecting me. Goosebumps, arm hairs standing on end, even a hitch in my breathing that was completely involuntary.

In short, it was pure torture.

When his thigh pressed against mine, I gasped, and although I tried to turn it into a cough, both Travis and Ander gave me suspicious looks. Grabbing my beer, I took a huge gulp, then slammed the bottle back down on the table. "We need more drinks." I hoped no one could hear the sudden hoarseness in my voice. How had I gone from simply thinking Liam was hot to being *this* affected by him?

Fuck my life.

"I'll get them. Another beer?" Travis climbed to his feet, placing his cards face down on the table. When he returned with an armful of beers, he slid two across the table in the direction of Liam and me. Liam took one of the beers and held out the other to me.

Our eyes met, and we were too close for comfort. He bit down on his lip as I took the bottle from him. The tips of his fingers touched mine, and I didn't miss his sharp intake of breath as his lashes lowered to hide his expression from me.

He's straight. This is all in your head. If I told myself enough, maybe I'd finally believe the words. False hope was a dangerous, dangerous thing. I'd been down that road before, and I had no intention of going back.

After the longest game in the universe, I managed to escape, making my way to my previous place, leaning against the kitchen counter and falling into conversation with Damon about one of our business professors, who had a reputation that he'd more than justified in our very first lecture, when he'd gone on a massive rant at one of the students in front of the rest of us. But even that wasn't enough to stop my attention straying to Liam, who'd also taken up his previous position opposite me.

Time passed.

I talked. I drank.

Liam did the same.

I looked at him, and he looked at me.

Then looked away.

Again. And again.

Until I'd emptied my sixth beer, tipping my head back to get all the dregs from the bottle. When I placed the empty bottle down on the counter, he was looking at me again, something dark in his gaze that sent heat straight through me.

My dick jumped. *Fuck.*

There was no way I was going to let another repeat of the gym happen, especially with so many people around. Without saying anything to anyone, I turned and headed straight out of the kitchen door and then legged it up the stairs to the safety of my bedroom.

"Noah."

I froze at the top of the stairs at the sound of the breathless rasp from behind me. Slowly, I turned to see Liam ascending the final few stairs until we were level. I took a step backwards, then another, till my back hit the wall behind me.

"What?" My voice was hoarse.

"Noah," he said again, closing the distance between us. "*Noah.*"

Fuck, just the way he was so close, breathing my name, had my dick so hard that I had to shove my palm down, attempting to make it less obvious.

"Liam?" I stared at him uncertainly. I didn't know if I was reading him right.

His eyes were wide, but the blue had almost been swallowed by his pupils.

"Fuck," he whispered, his breath hitting my lips, and then he planted his hands on the wall on either side of my face.

I didn't even dare to breathe.

Then, he kissed me.

And my entire world was turned upside down.

His lips. So soft, so hesitant at first, carefully brushing across mine. I let him lead. I couldn't even believe this was happening.

When he pressed incrementally closer, his chest lining up against mine so I could feel the rise and fall of his unsteady breaths, I let my hands slide around his neck and into his hair, keeping my grip light.

He made a low noise in his throat, tugging my bottom lip in between his teeth before releasing it. Then he licked across my lips, and that was enough for me. I angled my head forwards, kissing him back, and he opened his mouth for me. His hands came off the wall, going around the back of my neck as mine moved down his back. The kiss grew harder, deeper, his tongue licking into my mouth. My head was spinning—from the press of his lips against mine and the taste of beer on my tongue. The alcohol burned through my bloodstream, every nerve ending in my body alight, attuned to this man who was kissing me like he couldn't get enough.

Without a conscious thought, my hands gripped his ass, pulling him into me, and I felt his cock, rock-hard against my thigh.

"Oh, fuck," I groaned into his mouth, grinding my hips into his, angling myself so our cocks were aligned.

That was the moment it all went wrong.

His whole body went stiff, and he tore his mouth from mine, his eyes going impossibly wide and panicked.

I immediately released my grip on him. "Shit. Liam, I—"

But he was gone, his bedroom door slamming shut behind him, followed by the unmistakeable sound of the lock clicking into place.

THIRTEEN

LIAM

"*I*'m sorry. *There was nothing we could do.*"

The doctor's words hit me like a ton of bricks, and I crumpled into a ball on the floor. How could my dad have gone? He was supposed to be there for me. I was only seven; he couldn't leave me. He was supposed to be coming to watch me play in my first-ever football match. I'd just been accepted onto the school team, and he'd been so happy for me. He promised me he'd be there. He'd been so proud of me.

Dimly, I heard my mum's sobs, but I was lost in a black hole that I couldn't climb out of.

I woke with a gasp. Sitting up in bed, I rubbed at my eyes, breathing in and out slowly and steadily until my heart rate came down. I didn't dream about that moment much anymore, but when I did, it hit me all over again. I missed him, and I'd never stop missing him.

It had been the worst moment of my life. Losing my dad at such a young age—no one should have to go through that. One minute he was there, the next, gone.

It took a long, long time, but eventually, my mum and I found a new normal. There was an ache inside me that I knew would never go away, but things started to get easier to bear. One day, I realised that I'd smiled more than I was sad, and that was a comfort I hung on to.

"All he wanted was for you to be happy. One day, Liam, you'll be an adult. A man with a good job, a wonderful wife, and children of your own. And your dad will be so proud, smiling down on you."

My mum's words, repeated to me through the years as I grew up, never left me.

I'd finish university, get a good job, and find a girl to settle down with. That was what my dad would have wanted.

It was what *I* wanted.

The ball rebounded off the crossbar, and a frustrated sound escaped me. My concentration was completely shot today, not helped by the fact that I'd slept so badly.

A face flashed up in my mind. Dark, tousled hair, bright amber eyes, a sharp jaw topped with the lightest dusting of stubble, the softest fucking lips—

Fuck. Fuckfuckfuck.

Running down the pitch to intercept the ball, I did my best to get my head in the game, but my thoughts were too loud.

I'd had way too much to drink last night. That had to be the reason I'd acted so out of character. Noah and I were barely on the way to becoming friends, let alone anything else. And...no...that wasn't even relevant. What was relevant was the fact that *I was straight.*

Nineteen, almost twenty years I'd lived on this earth, and I'd never once been interested in guys. Any guys. *Ever*. Yeah, I could appreciate someone's looks without it meaning anything more, as I was sure most blokes could.

But how did I reconcile that with what had happened last night? How did I get my head around a kiss that had been leagues above any kiss I'd ever had in my life?

The sound of a whistle screeching close to my face brought me to a halt. I spun around, seeing Travis glaring at me.

"Liam! What the fuck! Pay attention." He jogged over to me. "What's your problem? You totally missed that cross from Levi. You're meant to be setting an example for the first years."

"I know. Fuck. Give me five," I ground out, already jogging towards the benches. There was no point in me being on the pitch in this practice session right now—I was a liability.

Seated on the sidelines, I kicked at the AstroTurf with the toe of my boot as Travis took the opportunity to swap out some of the other players, corralling the ones on the pitch into two teams. This day was going from bad to worse. After a night of tossing and turning, I'd woken up with a hard cock—not unusual, but it was very fucking unusual when it was accompanied by thoughts of my male housemate.

Fucking Noah. Ever since he'd driven into my car, he'd been messing with my head.

Travis blew the whistle again, and I finally managed to focus on what was happening on the floodlit pitch. The new guys were good—Levi, especially, which didn't surprise me because he'd been the captain of the football team at his school. Apparently, his boyfriend, Asher, was just as good—

not that I'd seen him play, but his all-expenses-paid appren-
ticeship to become a football coach clearly showed he had
talent.

I lost myself in the match for a while, noting down the
players' strengths and weaknesses so I could dissect them
with Travis later. We'd started doing it last year when
Travis had become the youngest captain the team had ever
had. Before he'd been picked, the captain had always been
one of the oldest players. After it had been announced that
he'd been offered and had accepted the position, we'd ended
up getting together with Preston and Ander once a week to
strategise. We wanted to be top of the universities' league.

When the final whistle blew, I headed into the changing
rooms with the others. As I soaped up my body in the showers, my thoughts went to the one person I didn't want to be
thinking about. Without permission, my mind replayed the
kiss, and my dick reacted. I slammed my hands onto the
white shower tiles, beyond frustrated. My brain needed a
fucking off switch.

If I was honest with myself, which I didn't want to be, it
had been building up before the kiss. Last night had just
been the culmination of whatever this was.

My hand lifted from the wall, slid over my abs, and
down to my rapidly hardening dick.

No.

I wouldn't let this happen. Not with Noah in my head,
and definitely not with my teammates in the shower stalls
next to me.

I finished up my shower as quickly as I could, my dick
finally deflating at the horrific thought of one of my teammates discovering my situation and, worse, somehow
reading my mind. There was no way I'd be able to explain
anything that was happening.

There was only one thing I could do. New plan: avoid Noah at all costs.

I managed to survive the rest of the day without any Noah sightings, and by the time I was ready to head up to bed, I'd made it a whole three hours without him invading my thoughts.

I had my foot on the bottom stair when I heard someone call my name. As I turned back, Damon came jogging out of the lounge, waving some papers at me. "Mate. Do me a favour if you're going up. Give these to Noah? He let me borrow them to take notes, but I know he needed them back tonight."

Fuck. There was no way I could refuse him without it seeming weird.

"Okay."

"Cheers." He shoved the papers at me and left. I groaned under my breath and made my way upstairs with the papers clutched in my hand.

When I reached Noah's door, my heart was hammering, and my palms were sweating. This was fucking ridiculous. I smoothed out the papers and eyed his door. Maybe I could just slip them under—

A low moan stopped my thoughts in their tracks. I froze in place, not even daring to breathe.

I heard a muttered "Fuck," followed by another moan, and before I was even aware of what I was doing, I was inching closer and pressing my ear to the door. My traitorous cock was hardening rapidly in my jeans at the thought of Noah, stretched out on his bed with his hand wrapped around his dick.

I couldn't be doing this. This was a violation of his privacy, and also, *why the fuck was I standing here listening to my housemate wanking?*

Dropping the papers to the floor outside Noah's door, I bolted for my room, locking the door behind me with shaking hands. Then I dived onto my bed, kicked off my jeans, and gave in to the urge I'd had on and off ever since I'd kissed him.

I got myself off to thoughts of Noah.

When I'd come in an absurdly short amount of time, the evidence striping my abs, I lay back with a groan, throwing my arm across my face as I tried to catch my breath. What the hell was I doing?

FOURTEEN

NOAH

There was no doubt about it. Liam was avoiding me again. I was around the house most of the following day since I only had two lectures, but he never showed up, even though I hung around in the communal areas late into the evening. The day after that was the same. He was gone when I got up and didn't appear again. I replayed Wednesday night over and over in my mind, but every time, I came to the same conclusion. He regretted the kiss. And why wouldn't he? The most likely reason for it happening in the first place was that it had been a moment of drunken curiosity. He wasn't even the first straight boy who'd kissed me out of curiosity.

I should have regretted it too. Not the kiss itself—but after everything that had happened in the past with Kyle and the football team, the last thing I wanted was to be caught in another situation with a boy who was either in denial or wanted to use me as an experiment.

I told myself this, but I couldn't stop thinking about Liam. The way he kissed...I'd *never* been kissed that way before. I wanted it to happen again, even though I knew I shouldn't.

"Noah? Shot?" Preston's voice startled me out of my thoughts. I accepted the tiny glass from his outstretched hand, leaning back against the kitchen counter.

Tonight, we were going to Revolve, the gay club. I had my doubts about whether Liam would even show, but I pushed those thoughts from my mind. Tonight was about having a good time in a place where I was completely free to be myself, where I could dance and maybe even flirt with other men without any worries in the back of my mind.

"No Liam?" I asked casually, before tipping my glass up. I grimaced at the sour taste of the alcohol as it burned its way through my body.

Preston's brow furrowed. "I haven't seen him today... maybe he changed his mind." He held up the bottle. "Another?"

"Why not." Holding out my shot glass, I watched as he filled it to the brim with clear liquid. "I haven't seen him around at all since Wednesday."

I kept my voice light, but Preston's frown deepened. "I haven't seen him around much either, other than at football yesterday, but I didn't get to speak to him. Last time I spoke to him properly was, uh—" He cleared his throat as Kian jabbed him in the ribs with his elbow. "—Wednesday night."

"When you ran out of the kitchen and he followed you, or so I heard. Anything you wanna share?" Kian interjected with a smirk on his face.

"Kian," Preston hissed. "It's none of our business."

"Nothing of note to share," I said, my cheeks heating. Downing my shot, I changed the subject. "Where is this club, anyway? Close?"

"It's in Soho," Preston informed me. He frowned, tugging his phone from his pocket. "The Uber's due in five minutes, and we're meeting Elliot and the other guys out front. Are we sure Liam isn't— Hey, man!"

I spun around at Preston's greeting to see Liam standing in the doorway. He was casual in jeans and a black T-shirt, but his hair was styled in an artful mess, and there was a resolute expression on his face.

"Everyone ready to go?" His gaze flicked from Kian to Preston, and he pointedly didn't look at me.

Okay, I could take a hint.

I made sure I went last when we headed outside, where Elliot and his friends were already waiting alongside the cabs. There were seven of us in total, so it meant that there'd be four of us in one of the cabs. Since Liam was ignoring me, I stepped around him, greeting Elliot. "Can I?" I pointed to the Uber his friends were getting into.

He grinned. "Yeah." Ducking his head into the cab, he spoke to the guys inside, and the next thing I knew, one of his friends was climbing out of the back and getting into the front. "Get in." He placed his hand on my back, applying a light pressure.

As I slid into my seat and Elliot climbed in next to me, I turned my head to see Liam staring straight at me with a look on his face that I couldn't quite interpret.

But it looked a lot like jealousy.

"Elliot." The bouncer tipped his chin at my friend as we stepped up to the roped-off entrance. He nodded back, going for extra casual, and it made me smile. Out of the corner of my eye, I could feel Liam's heavy stare, but I ignored it. I'd come here to have a good time, and I wasn't going to let anything bring my mood down. The atmosphere in the cab on the way had been happy, excited, all of us anticipating a good night. Elliot had given us a rundown of the club. It was spread out over three floors, and the entrance was on the middle floor, which played general dance, pop, and cheese, depending on the night's theme. Then up on the top floor, you had a huge chill-out section, and the music was more mellow. The basement was a completely different atmosphere, as Elliot described it. Dark, smoke machines, speakers pumping out grinding, dirty beats, and a long corridor leading to the toilets and doubling as a fire exit, which Elliot had flushed at when mentioning and then clammed up.

Suffice to say, I was intrigued.

We headed inside, straight for the bar. Once we'd shown our IDs, we were being introduced to Elliot's very hot cousin, Cole, and he was serving us a line of Jägerbombs followed by some other mixed drinks that definitely contained Red Bull and way too much alcohol. I was buzzing.

And I was very aware of Liam. Constantly checking him out to see if he seemed comfortable or whatever. Even though I knew he was avoiding me, I couldn't help myself. It was a weird, almost protective instinct, knowing he had to be way out of his comfort zone. Even here, on the main dance floor, there were guys plastered up against each other, grinding, attacking each other's mouths, hands every-where...my dick was half hard just from watching every-thing going on around me.

Liam seemed to be handling it just fine, though.

Until we went to the lower level.

I hadn't even been the one to suggest it. It had been

Preston, giving me a smile that was way too knowing, whispering in Kian's ear. It was no surprise that they both disappeared the second we'd made it down the stairs, melting into the crowds, the haze from the smoke machines camouflaging their exit.

Now I was stuck between Liam, who had gone from casually relaxed to stiff and uncomfortable, his wide-eyed gaze darting around the smoky room, and Elliot, who was staring at me in a way that I really hoped I was misinterpreting. Thankfully, Elliot's friends joined us a minute later, and I breathed a sigh of relief. Liam was still ignoring me, despite the fact that he was clearly out of his depth. Even I was, a bit... The nightlife back at home wasn't comparable to this.

The DJ crooned something into the microphone that I didn't catch because all my attention was focused on a gorgeous blonde girl who had sidled up to Liam, trailing her hand down his arm. How was it, even here in a gay club, he still managed to attract female attention?

Suppressing the unwanted jealousy, I made a snap decision, turning to Elliot. "Want to dance?"

His face lit up, and he held out his hand. "Fuck, yes."

Caught up in the sea of bodies, I lost myself in the beat. Elliot pressed up behind me, hands resting on my hips as we moved to the music. He angled his head forwards, his lips brushing my ear. His body ground against mine, our positions intimate, and yet...I felt nothing.

"He's watching us."

It took me a second to register Elliot's murmured words, but then I tilted my head towards him, my lips barely forming the words. "Who?"

"Liam," he breathed in my ear, his hands sliding from my hips to my stomach.

"W—what?" My gaze arrowed straight to the one place I'd been purposely avoiding looking at.

There he was. Illuminated by the club lights, a rainbow of colours sliding over his gorgeous body in a smoky haze, he commanded every single bit of my attention.

Completely ignoring the girl next to him, who now had her arm around the waist of another girl who was kissing down her neck, he was watching me intently, his fists balled up and his jaw clenched. A bright light swept across him, and I got a good look at his eyes in that moment. They were boring into me. So, so dark, and angry, and heated.

A sound escaped my throat that I hadn't even intended, and Elliot chuckled against me. "He wants you."

"He's straight," I protested.

"I thought so too until you came along." Elliot pressed closer to me. "Want to fuck with his head a bit?"

Angling my head further, I kept my eyes fixed on Liam. His gaze was burning into me, and it made my breath catch, my stomach flipping. "What do you mean?" Whatever Elliot's plan was, it had "bad idea" written all over it.

"What will he do if I do...this?" Elliot slid a hand up over my abs, up to my chest, while he nuzzled his nose into my neck.

I watched, fascinated, as Liam downed his drink, then slammed his glass down on the bar with such force that the guy on the other side of him jumped. He clenched and unclenched his fists, still staring at me, and I sucked in a sharp breath at the dark look on his face.

"My work here is done," Elliot murmured. "Maybe you can return the favour for me someday." Releasing his grip on my hips, he melted into the crowd.

I barely even noticed him leave.

There was nothing to lose. Lifting my hand, I crooked a finger at Liam, tilting my head in a silent invitation.

Time seemed to stand still.

Then.

He pushed away from the bar and stalked across the dance floor, straight towards me.

FIFTEEN

LIAM

I f I could think straight, I probably would've said something like, *What the fuck am I doing*? But all I could focus on was the fact that Elliot had his hands all over Noah, and no. Fuck. That.

Mine. Mine. *Mine.* The word resonated through me like a drumbeat, impossible to ignore.

Before I knew it, I was in front of Noah, his intense gaze focused on mine, filled with a hunger that I'd never seen on anyone before.

My dick jerked, the reaction to Noah as sudden and as unexpected as the first time it had happened. Setting my jaw, I pinned my arms to my sides, unwilling to do anything that would—

My brain went offline when Noah's hands went to my shoulders and he twisted me around, his body crowding up against my back. When his arms banded around my waist, and his head dipped to my ear, I forgot how to fucking breathe.

The bass vibrated through the huge space, low and

hypnotic, as Noah pressed into me, and I bit down on my lip, angling my hips away from him.

"Liam." His low hum in my ear vibrated through my skin, and I clamped my mouth shut to stop an involuntary noise from escaping.

"Liam," he said again. "What are you doing here?" There was a note of uncertainty to his voice, despite the confident way he was holding himself against me, and somehow, it made me more at ease.

"I don't know." My voice came out as a hoarse rasp.

"Hmmm." His lips skimmed across my neck, a trail of fire burning my skin. It felt so fucking good. "I think I do." The uncertainty was gone, and his hands went to my hips, moving us both to the heavy beat, his body grinding up against mine.

I stiffened involuntarily.

"Relax." His voice was soft and low against my ear as he moved back incrementally. "We're just dancing. Nothing else."

A shiver went down my spine. *Fuck.* This boy was going to kill me.

With an effort, I blocked any thoughts from my mind, concentrating only on the music and the slow roll of our hips. Right in front of us was a couple dancing in the same way we were, except the one guy was palming the other guy's obvious erection through his trousers. The other guy threw back his head against the first guy's shoulder, his eyes closed, his lip trapped between his teeth as the first guy put his mouth to his neck.

My dick jerked again. Fuuuuck.

Noah tugged me closer, and now the back of my body was completely flush with his front, both of us moving together in the same slow, sexy rolling movement that was starting to drive me insane. I could feel the unmistakable press of his hardness against me, and my breath stuttered. For one second, I wanted—I wanted him to do what the guy dancing across from us was doing.

The thought startled me so much that I stopped dead, right there on the dance floor. Noah gently nudged my hips, and I began to move again, my eyes falling closed. Why did this feel so fucking good?

When he began trailing his nose down the side of my face and onto my neck, I bit the inside of my cheek, hard, to stifle my groan.

He murmured against my throat, his teeth lightly scraping over my skin. "Earlier, were you jealous? Did you wish you were the one dancing with me?"

I couldn't fucking speak. It was so overwhelming.

"Tell me." He twisted me around to face him, planting his thigh between mine, and I sucked in a sharp breath, feeling the grind against my cock, which was rapidly hardening at the feel of him against me. It scared me just as fucking much as the last time it had happened, but this time, I didn't run from him.

He stroked his hands around my back, pulling me even closer. His lips traced another line of fire down my throat, and then he raised his head, his eyes meeting mine in the dim, pulsing club lights.

"Liam. Were you jealous?"

I swallowed hard. "*Yes*."

As soon as the word left my lips, I lunged for him, or maybe he lunged for me. All that mattered was getting his mouth on mine.

When he opened for me and I licked into his mouth, he let out a groan that went straight to my dick. My hands went around him, and although his body was lean, it was hard and muscled, and so different from a woman's. My fingers stuttered for a minute, making the connection, and then I was tracing over his back, feeling his muscles flexing under my hands. I forgot where we were, forgot the fact that we were surrounded by people who could see us, forgot everything except him.

He was the first to pull away, staring at me with his normally light eyes dark and wild, his fingers gripping the back of my neck. "Am I dreaming?"

I couldn't help my sudden laugh at his bewildered tone. "Dream about me a lot, hmm?"

"Maybe." Heat sparked in his eyes, and his gaze dropped to my lips. "Your fucking *mouth*," he groaned, going for me again.

My mouth? *His* fucking mouth. I'd never had a kiss like this in my life. All-consuming, obliterating my senses, making me want more, and more, and more.

Nothing else mattered except for the feel of his lips on mine.

The moment was broken when someone bumped into me, and my brain came back online, reminding me where we were.

Then the panic set in. My heart rate, already increased from the kiss, sped up even further. Shit, what if anyone we knew had seen us? What if they asked questions? How the fuck was I going to answer? I broke away from Noah, spinning around and heading in the direction of the corridor that I could see at the side of the room, over by the bar.

Big. Mistake. Really fucking big mistake. I turned a corner and stopped dead. Noah, who'd obviously followed me, ran straight into my back, sending us both staggering forwards before I regained my balance. Under the dim, blueish lights, I could make out the writhing bodies pressed up against the corridor walls, and the fucking noises coming from them…it was way, way too much.

"Fuck," Noah muttered, taking in my panic. His head twisted, and then he squeezed my bicep. "This way." His voice was decisive, and his hand on my arm was a reassuring weight. I let him lead me down the corridor and around another corner, and suddenly, fresh air was hitting my face.

He didn't stop, winding through the people grouped around the area, mostly talking, smoking, or drinking. When we reached the far side of the outdoor space, he glanced around us for a minute before dragging me into a corner, next to a small high wooden table with stools that were bolted to the floor.

I collapsed onto one of the stools, leaning my head back against the brick wall behind me.

"Better?"

The concern in his voice was clear, but I couldn't look at him. Now we were out in the open air, away from the heady atmosphere of the club, everything was crashing over me. I closed my eyes, gripping the sides of the stool in an attempt to ground myself.

"Liam." His hand brushed against my arm tentatively before dropping. "I'm sorry."

My eyes flew open. He was shifting on his feet, his dark lashes hiding his eyes from me as he stared at the ground.

What was I supposed to do now? He was messing with my head, but I couldn't let him take the blame. It wasn't his fault, and I'd been an active and willing participant in everything that had gone down between us. "Don't apologise."

"Yeah, but I shouldn't have pushed. I know you're not…" Trailing off, he shrugged, still staring down at the floor.

A loud clatter sounded next to us, and we both jumped. Noah's gaze darted to the left, then back, and his eyes finally met mine. He looked so distressed, I couldn't handle it. I sucked in a breath. "Look, let's just forget tonight happened, okay?"

His gaze shuttered. "If that's what you want."

The problem was, I didn't know what I wanted. I didn't know anything. It felt like my entire world had been turned on its head.

"It's what I want," I said, and I hoped he couldn't hear the lie in my voice.

SIXTEEN

NOAH

E xiting the taxi, I rubbed my hand across my face. I was back to square one with Liam again. After he'd told me to forget what had happened between us, he'd disappeared, presumably to get a cab home. I'd thrown myself into drinking and dancing with Elliot and his friends, but everything with Liam had kept replaying itself in my mind, and I'd struggled to focus on having a good time.

The way he'd kissed me—I'd never been kissed like that in my life. This inconvenient crush was in danger of turning into a full-blown obsession. I couldn't let it. Falling for a straight boy had heartbreak written all over it. Even if, based on the way he'd kissed me, I could almost convince myself he was into me, the shattered look on his face and the way he'd insisted that we forget what had happened told me the truth.

After he'd said those words to me, I was hurt, both for myself and for him, and yeah, I was a little angry too. The bottom line was—he didn't want me. He'd made that clear, and I knew it was for the best.

I needed to forget about Liam Holmes.

"Is everything okay?" Elliot gripped my arm, stopping me from walking up the path to my house. I stared at him. Did I tell him what had happened? Fuck, my life would be so much simpler if I was into him rather than Liam.

The sound of the black cab starting up behind us broke the silence that had fallen, and I sighed. I was drunk, tired, and I just wanted a friend to talk to.

"Not really."

He moved closer, pushing at my shoulder. "Come on. Inside. I've been told I'm a good listener, and you look like you could use it."

We ended up in the lounge, which was empty. Not really a surprise since it was almost four in the morning. Elliot sprawled out next to me, downing one of the pints of water I'd poured for us.

"Better," he murmured, dragging the back of his hand across his mouth. "Okay. Talk. This is about Liam, I take it?"

"Yeah." Kicking up my feet on the coffee table, I rolled my head to face him. "This needs to stay between us. I probably shouldn't even be telling you, but it's fucking killing me to keep it all inside." I couldn't out Liam, or whatever, and I wouldn't tell him about us kissing, but Elliot wasn't stupid. It was blatantly obvious he knew that something was going on between me and Liam based on his actions in the club.

"I wouldn't betray your trust like that," he assured me. "I'd like to think we're friends now."

"Yeah, we're friends." Shifting into a more comfortable position on the sofa, I closed my eyes, lowering my voice. "Okay. I'm into Liam, as much as I wish I wasn't. I wondered for a minute if he was into me too...but then tonight, he made it clear that he wanted to forget about us, uh, dancing together. Why do I have to be interested in him when I know it could never go anywhere? He's obsessed with football, which I hate, he's mostly into one-night stands, based on my observations and what other people have said about him, and there's also the fact that he's straight. No getting around that one."

"Being in love with a straight boy is the worst."

I raised a brow, taken aback by the vehemence in Elliot's tone. "Something you wanna tell me?"

He shook his head. "This is about you. Believe me, you don't want to hear about my fucked-up problems."

"I think I do." Intrigued, I leaned closer. "Maybe talking about it would help."

"It won't." Rubbing his hand across his face, he groaned. "But if we're confessing being into someone we really shouldn't be into, I'll admit to having a long-time obsession with my very gorgeous, very, very straight best friend. The best friend I now live with and have to see parade around in just his underwear and bringing home girl after girl right in front of me."

"Wait!" I shot upright as it hit me. "You're in love with *Ander*?"

"Fucking hopeless, aren't I? I do my best to forget about it. Flirt with cute boys like you, hoping that I'll finally get over him, but so far, nothing."

"Does he know?"

"Nope. Not a clue. He's completely oblivious, and I just hope it stays that way. I'm used to suppressing how I feel for him—most days, I can compartmentalise and just be a friend to him, but every now and then, it just gets too much, and I have to avoid him. He's good at giving me space, but I know it upsets him when I disappear. And it's hard to get space from someone when you live in the same house as them."

Liam seemed to manage it just fine.

I pushed that thought away. "Why are we drinking water? This conversation is way too depressing. Shots?"

"Shots."

When I returned with the bottle I'd been drinking from before the club and two shot glasses, Elliot climbed to his feet. "To getting over straight guys." We clinked glasses and downed the shots.

Then we had another, and another, and another, until the bottle was empty, and we passed out in blissful oblivion.

SEVENTEEN

LIAM

Nothing could have prepared me for what I saw when I walked into the lounge the next morning. The boy I'd spent the night trying to get out of my head was fast asleep on the sofa, his arm hanging off the side, his fingertips brushing against an empty bottle of what looked like vodka.

But it was how he was lying that made my breath catch in my throat. That, and the fact that he wasn't alone.

He was sprawled on his stomach, one leg hooked over Elliot's. If that wasn't bad enough, his left arm was draped across Elliot's stomach, and Elliot's arm was curled over his back.

They were fucking *cuddling*, and they looked way too comfortable doing it.

I guess our kiss hadn't meant anything to him, then.

Turning on my heel, I stalked out of the room, shoving my way past Travis, who had appeared in the doorway behind me. I ignored his exclamation of surprise, needing to get out of there before Noah woke up.

In the kitchen, I shovelled cereal into my mouth as fast as I could, ignoring Travis, who'd followed me into the kitchen, until he sat down on the bench opposite me with a loud thunk.

"What happened last night?" He stared at me.

"What do you mean?" I asked around a mouthful of cereal, playing dumb.

Drumming his fingers on the table surface, he raised a brow. "How about the way that I had to hear Kian throwing up when I walked past Preston's door just now, the fact that you look like someone pissed in your Cheerios, and then there's Noah cosying up with our neighbour in the lounge. I'll ask again, what the fuck happened last night?"

I was saved from replying by Damon's arrival in the kitchen, looking like he was still half asleep, rubbing at his eyes. "Preston wants to know if anyone has any painkillers." He snorted out a laugh. "Him and Kian are hungover as fuck."

"Yeah. Top cupboard, left-hand corner." Travis pointed a thumb in the direction of the cupboard, then turned back to me. "Explain."

"I don't know, okay? I left the club early. They were drinking before they went out; they must've overdone it. How the fuck am I supposed to know?"

A disappointed frown creased Travis' brows. "What about Noah and Elliot?"

Noah and Elliot. Noah and Elliot. The words played on a loop in my mind. I fucking hated them.

"Babe. Want a coffee?" Kira wandered in, leaning down to kiss the top of Travis' head. He reached out and caught her hand in his, pressing a kiss to it, then nodded. But he kept his gaze fixed on me, waiting for my reply.

"I don't know," I bit out through gritted teeth. "Why do you think I have all the answers? I know as much as you do, probably less."

Kira turned from her position in front of the coffee machine, eyeing us both with interest. "Who are you guys talking about?"

"Go and look in the lounge." Travis shot me a sly glance, and I glared at him.

A minute later, she'd returned, a beaming smile on her face. "Oh! They're so cute together. I'm so happy E's found someone as nice as Noah."

I wanted to slam my fist through a wall. Or maybe punch Elliot, even though he was a sort of friend. Well, he was Ander's best friend, and Ander was one of my close friends.

"You don't seem happy." Kira's attention was suddenly on me. I clenched my fist around my spoon.

"Ignore him. He's like that all the time lately." Travis took the mug of coffee Kira handed to him and then grinned at me. "I think he needs to get laid."

Kira's expression immediately turned sympathetic. "Aww, Liam. Want me to introduce you to some of the new girls? You haven't met Flick yet, have you? She's your type."

"I don't have a type," I muttered, scraping the last of the cereal from my bowl. Finally, I could escape my nosy housemate and his well-meaning but misguided girlfriend. I didn't need anyone pitying me.

Instead of heading straight up the stairs though, I did the worst thing I possibly could. I headed across to the lounge and peered around the door.

At first, I didn't see them. But then, as I moved to the left, they came into view. Noah was standing in the middle of the room, wrapped in Elliot's arms, his head buried in his shoulder.

My stomach churned. I didn't stop to see anything else.

Shoving my feet into my trainers, I got out of the house as fast as I could.

After wandering the streets of London aimlessly, I ended up at Southbank Skatepark, next to the river. Taking sips of the coffee I'd bought from a stall, I watched the skateboarders, my mind replaying everything. The way I'd reacted to the sight of Noah with Elliot—why did I hate it so much? Kissing him had been a mistake. Both times, there'd been alcohol involved—okay, at the club, I hadn't had much to drink, but the whole atmosphere of the place must've got to me. There was no way I could seriously be interested in him. It had to be pure curiosity. Didn't everyone have an experimental phase in uni?

I had to have imagined the way he'd affected me. His hot mouth, the way my dick had hardened against him, the way his body felt beneath my hands, so different to a girl's.

No good could come of this. He was obviously only looking for a bit of fun anyway. He'd moved on quickly enough. Soon the kisses we'd shared would be nothing more than a vague memory that could be explained away as a drunken, experimental moment.

By the time I'd finished my coffee and started heading back to the Mansions, my mind was made up. Noah was my housemate—nothing more, nothing less. I'd treat him like I did anyone else.

My plan went out of the window the second I stepped into the lounge and saw Ander there, holding a PS5 controller.

"Liam! Want a game? I was meant to be having a rematch with Noah, but he's over at my house right now, and I think he might be a bit busy with Elliot." He accompanied his words with a leer and an obscene hand gesture that was impossible to misinterpret.

I really needed to fucking punch something. Or someone.

"Can't. Sorry." Without waiting for a reply, I turned on my heel and legged it up the stairs to the safety of my bedroom. Fuck Elliot, and fuck Noah.

What were they doing now? Was Elliot getting to kiss those fucking soft lips? Did he have his hands on Noah's body, tracing those hard, flexing muscles, all defined from the gym and running? Was Noah's dick hard for him?

I shouted into my pillow, so frustrated that I couldn't help myself, then punched it twice for good measure.

Somehow after that, I managed to fall asleep.

Something had dragged me out of my dream. I blinked, disorientated. It was dark outside now. What had woken me?

The noise came again. Music, through my wall. The wall I shared with the bedroom next door.

Noah thought he could blast his music loud enough that I could hear it clearly in my room? I'd make sure he'd think twice about doing that again. Springing off my bed, I put my fist to the wall and pounded on it, hard.

"Turn your fucking music down, you wanker!"

Nothing happened for a minute, and then the music sounded even louder.

My fists clenched, and I growled under my breath.

This fucker was going to seriously regret pissing me off.

EIGHTEEN

NOAH

Waking up with a pounding head, thanks to my bad hangover and finding out I'd been using my friend as a pillow, didn't rate in the top ten of my favourite mornings. But Elliot had managed to take most of the awkwardness out of it. He'd just given me a grin and said he'd heard he made a comfortable pillow. Then he'd dragged me to my feet and hugged me, telling me that him confiding in me about Ander had been a real weight off his mind, finally being able to share his feelings with someone. I'd felt the same; even though I hadn't disclosed anything that had happened between Liam and me, just talking it through with him had made things a little clearer in my head. I felt lighter, knowing that he understood, given the situation he was in with Ander—which, in all honesty, was way worse than my situation.

In the spirit of friendship, I'd taken him up on his offer to go over to his house for food. We'd shut ourselves in his room, where he showed me a load of photos of him and Ander growing up, and then we'd watched some episodes of an anime show we were both into.

When I arrived back at my house, no one seemed to be around. I knew Preston had gone out somewhere with Kian, and Travis and Damon were nowhere to be seen. There was no noise coming from Liam's room when I pressed my ear to his door in a completely non-stalkerish way, so I assumed he'd gone out too. I knew I'd have to face him eventually, but I was glad for a reprieve.

After showering and changing into loose shorts and an old T-shirt, I flipped on the lamp next to my bed and connected my phone to my wireless speaker. Loading up Spotify, I hit Play on a random playlist, then crossed over to my desk, where I'd left the tin containing a half-smoked blunt that I'd saved from a couple of nights ago. When I'd hopped up onto the desk, I shoved the window open and lit the blunt. The pipes that ran behind my bedroom started gurgling loudly, so I increased my speaker volume. Smoke curled from the tip of the blunt as I leaned back against the wall next to the window, breathing in the evening air and making the most of this moment where I was alone. With two younger sisters and a sociable family, it was rare that I'd had time to myself in the past. I loved my family more than anything, loved the fact that everyone was welcome in our home, but having the house to myself had been a rarity.

My peace was suddenly shattered when there was a loud pounding on the wall, followed by an angry voice shouting, "Turn your fucking music down, you wanker!"

I guess Liam was home, then. And back to being pissed off with me, *again*.

There was only one thing I could do. As I took a slow drag of the blunt, I thumbed the volume control on my phone, increasing the level. Music poured out of the speaker, filling the room with a pounding, heavy bass.

Then I sat back and waited for the fireworks to begin.

It didn't take long before Liam was bursting into my bedroom, my door rebounding off the wall with a bang before slamming shut behind him. He glared at me, all bared teeth and fury in his eyes, and it was so fucking hot.

There had to be something wrong with me that I was finding his anger such a turn-on.

I gave him a lazy grin, holding up the blunt. "Want some?"

"You— No! I don't want your fucking weed. I want you to turn this fucking music down, *now*," he ground out.

"Make me."

As soon as the words were out of my mouth, he lunged for me, ripping the blunt from my fingers and launching it out of the window.

My shout of indignation died in my throat when he grabbed me and yanked me forwards to the edge of the desk, pressing his body between my legs.

"What happened between you and Elliot?"

Now he was all pressed up against me, growling in my face, spitting fire, and my dick was so fucking hard.

"*Nothing.*"

I didn't even get the whole word out before his mouth came down on mine.

This was nothing like the other kisses we'd shared. This was hard, angry, biting. He cupped the back of my head, his fingers digging into my skull as he held me in place. I let my arms go to his shoulders, sliding around to his back, and then I raked my nails downwards.

He moaned into my mouth, yanking me even closer, his hard cock rubbing against the inside of my thigh. The kiss turned less biting but no less frantic, both of us breathless and panting when he finally tore his mouth away.

"What...what was that for?" I leaned my forehead

against his, keeping a tight hold on him, my fingers flexing across his deltoids.

"Fuck. Noah." His voice sounded *wrecked*. He took a shaky breath, then tilted his head forwards, his mouth going to my throat as he angled my head to the side.

"Liam."

"Don't talk. Just..." Lifting his head, he slanted his mouth across mine again, pressing harder into me. When he pulled away this time, he released his grip on me and took one tiny step back, although he remained between my thighs. He planted his hands on the desk on either side of me, his darkened eyes meeting mine. "Elliot."

I knew what he was asking.

"Nothing happened. It's not like that. He's my friend, and I..." I trailed off, unable and unwilling to say the words aloud. *I'm only interested in you.*

He tugged his full bottom lip between his teeth, his brows pulling together as he studied me. My stomach flipped. He was so fucking gorgeous.

"I saw you with him," he said eventually. "This morning."

Oh. "Wanna know how I ended up like that? I had one of the best kisses I'd ever had in my life in the club last night. I thought maybe the guy was into me, but he said we should forget the kiss ever happened. He left, I got drunk, and Elliot was a shoulder to cry on. No, I didn't cry over you. That's just an expression," I added before he could make a comment. "Then shots seemed like a good idea at the time. We passed out drunk. It happens."

"Okay. Are you interested in him?" His voice was low.

"No." When his eyes narrowed, I sighed. I'd have to spell it out for him, even though I wasn't sure if this was a good idea based on the way he'd been acting around me and my own self-preservation instincts. "The *only* person I'm interested in is standing in front of me right now."

Leaning into me, he spoke against my lips, the barest brush of skin on skin. "Prove it."

Prove it? "How? You want me to get on my knees for you?" I said the words flippantly, but as soon as I said them, I heard his sharp intake of breath. Shock flared in his eyes, but it was immediately replaced with heat.

He licked his lips, and then nodded slowly. "If that's how you want to convince me, yeah."

My heart pounded, and I tried not to let my own shock show on my face as he drew back a little, but he smirked at me. Guess I hadn't hidden it as well as I'd hoped.

"What's the matter? Scared?" he taunted, but then his expression turned uncertain. "Or don't you want—"

I clapped my hand over his mouth, feeling his grin under my palm. When I removed my hand, I gave him a quick, hard kiss. "Oh, I want to. I just wasn't expecting that you'd want me to."

"Scared, then, huh?"

"Fuck off." Pushing off the desk, I gripped his shoulders and twisted us round so he was against the desk and we were standing chest to chest. Releasing Liam's shoulders, I traced down the lines and bumps of his torso. I stopped when I hit the top of his loose navy jogging bottoms. "Last chance to back out."

In response, he bared his teeth at me. "Get on with it." The effect was undermined by the fact that his voice had become a hoarse rasp that went straight to my dick.

Biting back a smile, I lowered my hand to his cock. At the first touch, he hissed, bucking into my hand. I stroked up and down his length over the fabric before dropping to my knees. My fingers went to his waistband, and I tugged his joggers down, his gorgeous, hard cock springing free.

Precum was already beading at the tip, and my mouth watered. I couldn't believe he was letting me do this, but now he was, I was going to give him the best blowjob he'd ever had. For a second, in the back of my mind, I wondered if this was a good idea, but I shook it off. The raw need in Liam's eyes was enough to blow any doubts out of the water.

Gripping the base of his cock, I leaned forwards, flattening my tongue and dragging it across the head. His groan made my dick throb, but I ignored that. There'd be time to get myself off later.

I licked all around the head, teasing him while my free hand rolled his balls. Taking a risk, I slid a finger back to press against his taint. He tensed for a second, but then when I did it again, he moaned, and I took that as approval. Keeping my touch light, I continued teasing the head of his cock with my lips and tongue until one of his hands buried itself in my hair and tugged.

Raising my eyes to his face, I found him staring down at me, his lips all shiny and bitten, and his gaze dark and hot. The hand that wasn't in my hair was gripping the edge of the desk so hard that his knuckles were turning white. "Noah. Fuck. *Please*."

My breath caught in my throat at his "please." Lowering my head again, I closed my mouth around his cock, taking more and more of him in until he hit the back of my throat. Then I got into a rhythm, slow and dirty, my tongue teasing him every time I pulled back, humming around his length and swallowing around him when I bottomed out.

He was a mess above me, all gasps and pants and breathy moans of my name, his fingers tightening in my hair as his thighs shook against my shoulders. The head of his cock repeatedly hit the back of my throat as I increased my pace, feeling his balls drawing up, and then his cock pulsed in my mouth and he was coming down my throat. He was so deep that I barely even tasted him, swallowing around his length until he tugged my head again. I couldn't help giving him one last lick when he'd withdrawn from my mouth, catching the final drops of his cum on my tongue.

I blinked several times, my vision blurry from the tears filling my eyes. When I finally staggered to my feet, Liam had tucked himself back into his trousers, and he was staring at me with wide eyes, his breaths still coming in pants.

A wide, satisfied grin curved over my lips. "Good?"

He huffed out a heavy breath, attempting an annoyed look, although it was half-hearted at best. "You know it was." His gaze darted down to the obvious outline of my hard dick. An apprehensive look crossed his face, and I quickly shook my head.

"I need a shower."

The relief in his eyes was evident, but I didn't take any offence at it. I could guarantee that his head was spinning, and not just because I'd sucked his brains out of his dick. The ball was in his court. He knew I was gay, and he knew I liked him.

It was up to him what he did with that information.

NINETEEN

LIAM

Bleary-eyed and stifling a yawn, I glanced at my phone screen. Only nine-fifteen in the morning.

I hadn't even fallen asleep until sometime after 4:00 a.m. My head had been too full, going over everything that had happened with Noah, the way he made me feel, and attempting to line it up with everything I thought I knew about myself.

I'd come to a few conclusions. One: Noah was a fucking master at kissing. Two: he gave the best blowjob I'd ever had in my life, bar none. Three: I was attracted to him. There was no doubt in my mind.

Point number three, and everything else that came with it, was way too hard to get my head around, and I had an essay due on Monday that I hadn't even started yet. It was one I needed to do well on—it counted towards my final grade for the module, and my professor was an absolute bastard. He didn't tolerate anything that didn't have 100 percent effort put into it, and he seemed to get a sadistic pleasure from tearing people down in his lectures. So for now, I needed to somehow find a way to push everything with Noah to the back of my mind so I could get this essay banged out.

But first, coffee.

After throwing on a pair of shorts, I made my way downstairs and into the kitchen, still yawning. It was empty except for the person who'd been occupying my thoughts for most of the night. I took a minute to appreciate the lines of his bare back, going down to the tempting curve of his ass that was currently covered by a pair of long black shorts. Below the shorts, the muscles of his calves flexed as he shifted from one bare foot to the other, tapping his fingers on the counter as he waited for the kettle to boil.

Fuck. It was like he had a direct line to my cock. How and when had this happened?

I swallowed hard, then cleared my throat.

Noah spun around, a smile on his face that died away when he saw me. He sucked his lip between his teeth, giving me a hesitant look.

"Hi." Crossing the room to stand against the same counter, I reached for my mug, then grabbed a pod for the coffee machine.

"Hi. Are you..." Pausing, he took in my appearance, and his brows furrowed. "You look tired."

I shrugged. "Didn't sleep well." Slotting the pod into the machine, I placed my mug under the nozzle, and I almost missed the way his face fell.

"Oh." He turned away from me, and his whole body was so stiff. I'd bet anything that he'd taken my comment the wrong way, thinking it was to do with him. Yeah, okay, it *was* to do with him, but not in the way he was probably imagining.

A sudden weird urge came over me, and I followed it through without even thinking about it. Stepping up right behind him, I planted one arm on the counter and wrapped the other around his waist. Then before he had a chance to react, I angled my head forwards and clamped my teeth down on the top of his shoulder.

"Hey!" Shaking me off, he spun around with a savage glare, although it was clear he was trying not to laugh. "What was that for?"

"Punishment for you playing your music too loud yesterday." I smirked at him.

"What are you, five? Who bites someone as punishment?"

I stepped up to him, gripping the counter on either side of his body. His eyes darkened as I lowered my mouth to his shoulder, skimming my lips across his warm skin. "Can you really call it punishment if you liked it, though?"

"Liam. You—"

He didn't get to finish whatever he was going to say because we both heard the stairs creak. I sprang away from him, busying myself with the coffee machine, hitting the button to start it up. Out of the corner of his eye, I saw him scrub his hand across his face, and his hand went to his shorts, subtly adjusting himself. Thank fuck the thought of one of our housemates discovering us in a compromising position had made my cock deflate almost instantly.

Travis stumbled into the kitchen with Kira under his arm, both of them looking as tired as I felt. Kira raised a hand in greeting and then took a seat at the table.

Travis stepped over to Noah, a sly grin on his face. "No Elliot this morning?"

Grabbing my mug from the machine, I gritted my teeth in a sudden murderous rage.

Calm the fuck down.

"That was...nothing happened. We're just friends."

Noah shot me a sideways glance before picking up his mug of tea and heading over to the kitchen table to join Kira.

"But you want it to be more, right? You two looked so cute together." Kira's smile was soft as she looked at Noah, and I couldn't handle it.

Not bothering with a goodbye, and definitely not waiting to hear whatever Noah's reply was, I walked straight out of the kitchen and into the lounge, slumping down on the sofa across from Damon. He was oblivious as always, AirPods in, doing something on his laptop.

What was I doing, messing around with Noah? Everyone seemed to have a hard-on for Elliot with him. Elliot, as much as I didn't want to admit it, was a nice guy, and everyone liked him. He was one of those studious types without being a geek. He shared interests with Noah; they were always doing running shit together. I could objectively see that Elliot was a good-looking guy, and most importantly, he was gay.

I was good-looking enough, but none of the other things applied to me. Noah deserved to be with someone who'd treat him right, who was sure in their sexuality and would be happy to be seen with him. Not this weird thing we had going on now with all the back-and-forth, hidden kisses, and me jumping away from him when there was a danger of anyone catching us.

The problem was I didn't want to do the right thing. I couldn't admit it out loud, but I wanted Noah for myself.

Stuck in the library, up on the sixth floor, hidden away in a corner next to the window, I rubbed at my temples. My essay was mostly done, other than the bibliography—thank fuck, because I was getting a headache. Not to mention, it was getting late. The sky outside was dark, and the library was quiet.

The words blurred on my laptop screen as I typed the name of the first book on the list, and I blinked rapidly, stifling a yawn.

"You should get some rest."

My head shot up to see Noah eyeing me with concern.

How had he found me?

"What are you doing here?" The words came out harsher than I'd meant them to because he took a step back, holding up his hands.

"No need to bite my head off. I wanted to..." He trailed off, pulling out the chair next to me and lowering himself into it.

"Take a seat, why don't you."

"Thanks, I will." He smirked, so I gave him the finger.

Resting his elbows on the table, he pushed his chair back a bit, then slumped forwards, laying the side of his head on his arms so he was facing me. His eyes raked over me, and his lips parted, his tongue coming out to swipe along his bottom lip.

This fucker knew exactly what he was doing. "Comfortable?" Playing it cool, I raised a brow before turning back to my laptop. I wasn't going to give him the satisfaction of knowing just how his proximity was making my heart rate speed up, and I was going to have a dickuation if he didn't stop looking at me with that heavy-lidded gaze, banked heat in the depths of his eyes.

"Mmm. Very." Shifting incrementally, he angled his body closer to me. "Why did you run out of the house this morning? Was it what Travis and Kira were saying about Elliot?"

My gaze snapped back to his. "What?"

"Because I already told you, nothing happened with Elliot, and I'm not interested in him as anything other than a friend," he continued as if I hadn't spoken. "Travis and Kira don't know what they're talking about. Anyway, after you'd gone, I told them that there was nothing going on, and—"

"You didn't tell them about me, did you?" Sudden panic had me flying up in my seat.

"No, I didn't. I wouldn't do that." Hurt crept into his tone, and he turned his gaze away from me, resting his chin on his arms and staring straight ahead of him.

"I know. I just...fuck." It was easier to say this now he wasn't even looking at me. "Maybe you should think about you and Elliot." I forced the words out through gritted teeth. "He's a nice guy, he clearly likes you, and he's, y'know."

"Gay?" Noah's voice was resigned.

"Yeah. I'm not... You and me...we don't even have anything in common. You hate football, I hate running unless it's on the pitch, we—"

"Is it me you're trying to convince or yourself, Liam?" Noah straightened up, getting into my personal space. His voice lowered. "If you're not interested in me, stop making excuses. I'm not interested in playing games."

"I'm not—"

He held up a hand, cutting me off again. "I get it. No need to say anything else." Before I had a chance to say anything else, he shoved his chair back and stalked away from me.

Fuck this boy. Why wouldn't he let me finish speaking? I shoved my own chair back and ran after him, grabbing his arm and yanking him into the stacks. Clapping a hand over his mouth to stop him from interrupting me again, I used my body to hold him in place against the shelves, my other hand holding the shelf at the side of his head.

"Let me speak without you fucking interrupting me and second-guessing what I'm going to say, alright?"

He tried to say something, so I pressed my hand harder against his mouth, digging my fingers into the sides of his jaw as a warning. His eyes narrowed in a glare, but he finally nodded.

"Good. What I was trying to say was—" I paused, taking a second to gather my thoughts. Noah shifted against me, but he didn't try to speak again. "I don't—we're not—we don't share the same interests. It's not just about that either. I'm... I know I'm not always that easy to get on with. To be completely fucking honest, I don't even know why you're interested in me. There's nothing I can offer you. Why would you want to be with me? I'm not out—fuck, I don't even know if I'm straight like I always thought I was, and this whole thing is a blip or something, or if there's some shit about me that I never realised before. I can't—"

Noah's hand came up, his fingers curling around my palm and pulling it away from his face.

"Yeah, I'm interrupting you again. Get over it." He lowered his hand, still keeping hold of mine. I was suddenly aware of the unsteady rise and fall of his chest and the way the hand that gripped mine had the slightest tremor. "I just want to ask one question, and I want you to give me an honest answer."

His eyes met mine. Angling his head forward, he spoke in a whisper. "Are you interested in me, Liam?"

I couldn't fucking speak. There was a moment of silence when it felt like all the air had been sucked out of the room, and then, finally, I gave a single nod.

"Good," he breathed, and then his lips were on mine.

He let go of my hand in favour of sliding his arms around my waist, so I brought my hand up to cup the back of his neck, my fingers brushing across the short hairs there. He shivered, and I smiled against his mouth.

His lips moved to my ear. "Why don't we try doing some stuff together?"

I pressed into him, getting one of my thighs between his. My brain had forgotten all the arguments I'd been having with myself now his body was all up against mine. "Mmm, yeah. I like this idea."

"Not that." Drawing back enough to look at me properly, he gave me a small smile. "I mean, what you were saying about us having nothing in common. Why don't we try spending some time together, as friends? Go out somewhere, or whatever. There's more to life than running and football, you know."

"More to life than football?"

He rolled his eyes at my pretend shock. "More to *us* than running and football, then."

The thump of a book being dropped sounded from a couple of stacks over, and we both jumped. He quickly released me, and I stepped back until I hit the shelves behind me. My heart was pounding, but I managed to reply. "Okay."

"Okay." Pushing away from the stack he was leaning against, he made his way to the end of the aisle. "Did you realise you left your laptop unattended out here? Someone could've nicked it."

"If you hadn't run off when I was trying to have a conversation with you, it wouldn't have been left unattended. If anything, it's your fault." I followed him back over to the desk where I'd left all my stuff.

Lowering his voice, he leaned into me. "Yeah, but if I hadn't, I wouldn't have been able to kiss you in the library."

I glanced around us. I couldn't see anyone in our immediate vicinity, so I twisted my head and brushed a quick kiss across his lips. "You were saying?"

He smiled, wide and happy. "Why don't you finish whatever you're doing? I'll go and grab us some coffees from the third floor." I was already sliding into my seat and moving my laptop into place as he was speaking, and I nodded in agreement. Taking a step away from me, he hesitated for a second, then came back to me, bending down to place his mouth to my ear. "When you're finished, maybe we can go back home and try doing some *stuff* together."

"Fuck," I muttered, shifting in my seat. He straightened up, giving me a cocky grin, then strutted away in the direction of the doors without a backwards look.

It was a good job there was no one around to see the shameless way I checked him out, adjusting my cock as he walked away from me.

TWENTY

NOAH

My plan to get Liam alone in either his bedroom or mine had been thwarted the second we'd walked in the door and Travis had accosted us and dragged us both into the lounge, announcing it was pizza and film night. Elliot was there, seated next to Ander, with a free space on his other side. Liam had immediately stiffened next to me when he'd seen him, and I knew he was still sensitive about the whole situation, even though I'd assured him that the only thing I felt for Elliot was friendship. So I made sure to give Elliot a polite smile before sitting on the other sofa, right in the middle, so Liam would either have to sit next to me or Elliot.

Elliot had given me a knowing look, the corners of his mouth tugging upwards, and I had to bite down on my lip to hide my own smile. I was fairly confident about which seating option Liam would pick, but when he immediately collapsed right next to me, I couldn't hide my smile any longer. I needed to get a fucking grip before anyone noticed the weird way I was acting.

More and more people piled into the lounge, crowding

around the TV, taking up seats on the arms of the chairs, and dragging in beanbags and cushions from other rooms. All our housemates, most of the guys from next door, and all the rest of the football team were here. We ended up with four people on a sofa that was really only designed for three, meaning I got to get up close and personal with Liam without anyone thinking anything of it. The line of his body pressed against me was warm, and all I wanted was to be alone with him.

Something in the back of my brain prodded at me—reminding me that I'd been down this road before—sneaking around in secret. But how could I explain how different this felt? The way I reacted to Liam...the way he reacted to *me*...

I didn't want to stop.

"You owe me a blunt," I told him in a low voice, just so I had an excuse to lean closer. He grunted in reply, his gaze fixed on the TV screen, but his little finger stretched out to stroke across the side of my thigh, out of view of the others.

Butterflies. That was what he gave me.

On-screen, there was a series of explosions, almost deafening through the soundbar. Liam used the moment to turn his head the tiniest bit. His breath caressed my skin as his soft rasp sounded in my ear, too low for anyone else to hear.

"After this, you're mine."

Fuck.

The movie that was supposedly two hours and eleven minutes long lasted approximately seventeen hours. And as much as I appreciated that everyone was together, a group of friends hanging out, just the way I'd hoped for when I'd thought about what uni life might be like, I wanted to be alone with Liam.

When the credits finally rolled, I was up and out of my

seat before I registered that everyone was staring at me. I didn't dare to look down at Liam, whose shoulders were shaking with suppressed laughter. *Bastard.*

"In a hurry?" Travis raised a brow at me.

"Uh, I'm going to...phone my mum."

"At midnight?"

"Look at his guilty face! Bet he's going to watch porn—"

"—have a wank."

There was way too much laughter going on at my expense, and I stuck my finger up at the room in general as I backed towards the door. "Just for the record, I hate you all."

"For someone who hates football, your housemate's alright," I heard as I headed down the hallway. It made me smile.

My phone buzzed with a text when I reached the second-floor landing.

Hot Angry Boy: Give me 30 mins

Another half an hour, after I'd just been through over two hours of torture, seated next to him but not able to touch? Even more torture. But I could make it appear like I wasn't dying waiting for him.

Me: OK

I filled the time by jumping in the shower, resolutely ignoring my half-hard dick. When I was done and I'd finally calmed myself down, I pulled on a T-shirt and loose shorts, not bothering with underwear, then collapsed back onto my bed and wasted time playing games on my phone.

The knock on my door came thirty-two minutes later, not that I was counting.

I threw the door open, letting Liam into my bedroom. Instead of going for me, he pressed something into the palm of my hand, then strolled past me to stand in the centre of the room. Looking down at my hand, I saw he'd brought a sloppily rolled joint with him.

"Replacement for your blunt. It was the best I could do at short notice—had to nick some weed from Ander's stash. I had to tell him I needed it tonight to help me sleep, so you'd better appreciate it."

My heart skipped a beat, and a helpless smile spread across my face. "Some boys bring me flowers, but you had to go one better. Although, technically, you owed it to me anyway."

He returned my smile. "It's the thought that counts. Did you want flowers?"

"Nah, I'm not really a flowers kind of guy. Give me weed any day." Hopping up onto my desk, I cracked the window open. "You wanna smoke this now?" Anticipation thrummed between us, but suddenly I wanted to draw this out, despite my earlier impatience. Liam was here now, and neither of us was going anywhere. I trusted that he wouldn't run this time, not when he'd shown up here of his own volition.

He replied by rifling through my desk drawer, grabbing my lighter and ashtray.

I eyed him suspiciously. "How did you know those were there?"

"Lucky guess." Shooting me a blinding smile, he handed me the lighter. I lit the end of the joint and inhaled, and then before I had a chance to react, he was parting his lips and pressing them to mine, so I exhaled into his mouth.

"Mmm." I drew back. "I like this."

"My turn." Taking the joint from my hand, he inhaled, then sealed his mouth over mine. My arms went around his waist, tugging him to stand between my legs, and then we were properly kissing, tongues sliding together, all hot and wet and smoky from the weed. He broke away for a second to dump the joint in the ashtray, and then his mouth was back on mine, kissing me harder as his hands came down to grip my hips.

"Noah." His lips moved to my jaw, kissing along it. My dick throbbed in my shorts, hard and ready for him, and I pulled him even closer, needing the friction of his body against mine.

Raising his head, he scooped his hands under my legs and lifted me, staggering backwards at the sudden weight, sending us both flying onto my bed. If the bed hadn't been behind the desk, we would've both hit the floor. "Fuck, you're heavy."

"Well, yeah. We're almost the same size." I buried my sudden grin in his neck, but he must've picked up on my tone because he tugged on my hair, hard.

"Shut up."

All my humour died away when I shifted against him, and suddenly our dicks were lined up, and he was gasping against me.

"You like that?" Raising my head so I could see his face, I ground down on him. His eyes lowered, his thick lashes sweeping down, as his mouth fell open on a low groan that felt like it sent vibrations all the way down to my cock.

"Liam." I lowered my face to his ear. "Is this okay? Do you like it?"

"Yeah," he rasped. "Fuck, yeah."

Good. As much as I wanted him, if he hadn't been comfortable, I would've backed off straight away.

But we should probably talk about this, regardless. "Li—"

"I thought. I told you. To shut up." Punctuating his words with hard kisses, he rolled us over on the bed so I was underneath him. Then he kissed me again, sliding his tongue into my mouth and grinding his hips against mine.

"Bossy," I muttered against his lips, which caused him to lift his head and flash me a sudden grin.

"You might be the one with experience with guys, but don't make the mistake of thinking you're the one in charge."

"Oh, really?" Raising a brow, I shot him a challenging look. "Show me what you've got."

He pushed off me, moving backwards and off the bed, and I let myself appreciate the sight of his gorgeous body and the huge tent in his shorts that told me he was just as into this as I was. He shut my door and locked it, then stood there, staring at me. Heat flared in his gaze when I licked my lips and beckoned to him.

His voice came out low and throaty. "I hope you're ready for this."

I was more than ready. "Oh, I am."

TWENTY-ONE

LIAM

There was no turning back this time. I knew I'd confused Noah with the way I'd been acting around him—but I didn't know if he realised just how confused I'd been myself. But after our conversation in the library earlier, cemented by our mutual decision to be here together, right now, I was all in. All I wanted was to lose myself in him, to make him forget anyone's name but mine.

I allowed myself to finally look at him properly, to give in the way I'd wanted to, ever since that night I'd seen him kissing that blond dickhead at the party. I'd buried that desire deep down, denied it to myself, but now I let myself feel the burning attraction that had come out of nowhere and completely blindsided me, just like the way we'd first met when he'd crashed into my car. Seeing him there, sprawled out on his bed, mine for the taking, made my dick rock-hard and my heart race. He was so fucking gorgeous. His deep brown hair was all mussed up from where I'd had my hands in it, his cheeks were flushed, and his amber eyes were dark and wide. His soft lips were reddened from the way we'd been kissing, and it made me want to kiss him even more.

Last time we'd been in a similar position, after he'd given me a blowjob, I'd been apprehensive and unsure, but the large bulge in his shorts didn't deter me this time. It was the opposite. I wanted to look, to touch, to taste. Fuck, I just wanted to mess him up, to make him as wrecked as I was already feeling.

"T-shirt off."

A smile curved over my lips at the way he instantly obeyed my command. This was a side to him that I hadn't seen before, and I liked it. A lot.

"Are you going to come over here, then?" He spoke hoarsely, staring at me from beneath his lashes as he ran a hand down his torso, flexing his muscles as he did so.

Fucking tease.

My cock was so hard, just watching him, and I had to fight my instincts and force myself to stay where I was.

"Shorts off."

One eyebrow flicked up. His tongue slid across his lips as his fingers curled around the waistband of his shorts. "If that's what you want." Then, he began to lower them, and it took me 2.5 seconds to realise that he wasn't wearing anything underneath.

I swallowed hard as his erect cock was revealed, the proof of just how aroused he was.

For me.

Lifting a finger, he beckoned me, like he'd done at the club. "Come here."

I was just as powerless to resist as I'd been then.

But still, I took my time, drawing out the moment. Despite the fact that I was 80 percent confident, the other 20 percent of me was pure nerves. I needed that time to regroup, to remind myself that even though I'd never done this before, Noah was obviously into me, and I knew how to make it good for people that were into me. It was all about reading their body language, and that was something I liked to think I was good at. Plus, the longer I waited, the more riled up Noah would get.

Lowering my hands to the hem of my T-shirt, I watched as his gaze tracked my movements, his pupils dilating even further as I lifted it, pulling the fabric up my body. The way he was looking at me...it was like he'd looked at me in the club, like no one had ever looked at me before.

When my T-shirt dropped to the floor, I took a step towards the bed. Then another. When my legs hit the edge of the mattress I stopped, taking a second to breathe.

"Liam."

My name was hissed out between his teeth, his fingers clenching and unclenching at his sides as he forcibly restrained himself from reaching out. I took one long, sweeping glance down his body, and fuuuuck...yeah, I *really* liked what I saw.

I lowered my shorts, taking my underwear with them. The cool night breeze that was snaking into the room from the still open window stroked across my skin, sending goose-bumps popping across my arms. Or maybe it was the way Noah's gaze was so fucking ravenous as he took in my body, bared to him.

There was nothing between us now.

Noah made a low, desperate noise in his throat, and that was *it*.

I lunged for him.

When my body covered his and he surged up to kiss me, I was lost. His arms wrapped around me, and his legs tangled with mine, and any doubts I'd had about this feeling weird were wiped away. His body against mine felt so right.

"Liam," he panted in my ear, "tell me what you want."

Instead of replying, I rolled my hips down. The hot slide and friction of his cock against mine felt so good, but I needed more. He was moaning underneath me, his hips moving against mine, his head thrown back against the pillow, baring his neck to me.

I took advantage, dragging my teeth over his skin and then clamping down. A gasp fell from his throat, followed by the dirtiest low moan I'd ever heard in my life.

"Lube. Drawer." His words were strangled, but I still made them out. Shifting on top of him, I fumbled for the drawer, getting it open and finding the bottle on the first try. When I passed it to him and moved back into position, he looked up at me, smoothing one hand down my back. "I need to know what you want."

"I want to fuck you." The words came out without thought, but they were true. We'd gone from zero to a hundred, but I wanted it. There was no doubt in my mind.

"I don't think—" He bit down on his lip, and I had to kiss him. He groaned, opening his mouth for me, his tongue sliding against mine. But then he stopped me by moving his hand from my back to my jaw and gripping it, pushing gently. "Fuck. I can't think when you're kissing me."

"Is that a problem?" Our faces were still close together, our breaths mingling, sweet and smoky from the weed. I lightly brushed my nose against his, and he huffed out a soft breath.

"No, it's... This isn't... I don't want this to be something we rush into. Something you regret."

Maybe he was right, but I wanted to fuck him more than I'd ever wanted to fuck anyone in my life. But I wouldn't push him if he thought we should wait. "Okay. What do you want to do?"

"I've got an idea." Releasing his grip on my chin, he pumped some of the lube into his hand, warming it between his fingers. He shifted me off him, so I ended up on my side next to him on the bed, and reached down between his legs.

I stared down between us. "What are you—" My words were cut off when he wrapped his hand around my cock. "Oh, fuck. *Yes*."

His thumb brushed over the head, smearing the precum with the lube, and I groaned, my cock jerking in his grip.

I had to touch him.

Reaching out, I curled my fingers around his erection, swallowing his gasp as I slanted my mouth across his. A slow slide of my hand, up, then down, and my confidence grew. I settled into an easy stroking motion that he seemed to be really into based on the way he was thrusting into my hand and panting breathless moans against my lips.

Then he tore his mouth away and grabbed my wrist, stilling it. "No. Wait. Fuck, Liam, you make me lose my mind. I want to try something. I want this to be good for you."

"It *is* good for me." Still, I released his cock and watched as he rolled onto his stomach.

"I think I'm developing a back fetish," I told him, straddling him and tracing a line of kisses down his spine. He laughed into the pillow, then turned his head to the side.

"Put your dick between my legs."

An amused grin curved over my lips as I complied. "No one's ever said that to me before. How can I say no to an offer like that?" When I was in place, my body lined up with his, my elbows planted on either side of him and my cock between his legs, I lowered my head and whispered in his ear, "Now what?"

"Now..." He shifted, his legs coming together, and my cock was suddenly trapped in tight heat between his thighs, slicked up with lube. "You move."

Fuuuuck. I knew that when he finally let me fuck him, it would feel different, but this right now? This was so. Fucking. Good. My dick slid along his ass and taint, my cockhead tapping against his balls as I thrust my hips in a slow, rolling movement. His body was hot and hard beneath me, his ass pushing back into my thrusts. I nipped at his shoulder, and he rewarded me with one of those dirty low moans that went straight to my dick.

"I'm not gonna last," I panted against his ear, and he moaned again.

"Come for me. I want to feel it."

His words tipped me over the edge I'd been balancing on. My whole body shuddered as my cock throbbed, and I came so hard that my vision was whiting out around the edges.

I collapsed against his back, breathing hard. "Fuck. *Fuck.*" That was the only word I could manage.

He shifted beneath me, huffing out a laugh. "Good?"

My brain finally rebooted, and I realised something. "You haven't come yet, have you?"

"Don't worry about me." His words were mumbled into the pillow, but they were clear, and yeah, no. Like fuck was he going to come away from this unsatisfied.

I placed an open-mouthed kiss to his shoulder, the salty tang of his warm, smooth skin so good that I had to kiss him again. Then again. Eventually managing to tear myself away, I moved onto my knees, straddling him. "Turn over."

When he turned to lie on his back, my breath caught in

my throat. His cock was so hard, dripping precum onto his stomach. His face was flushed, and his pupils were completely blown as he stared up at me.

"What do you want?"

He bit his lip. "I...had a fantasy. Of you..."

"Of me what?" Gripping his cock, I stroked my thumb over the head, and he moaned, arching into my hand.

"*Liam*." Lifting his hand, he traced his finger across my lips before lowering it. "Of—of your lips stretched around my cock."

Fucking hell.

"Yeah, okay. I can do that." My voice came out hoarse.

"You don't have to do anything you don't want—"

"I know. I want to." Before I could overthink it, I moved into position, lowering my head, and took his cock into my mouth.

He let out a choked moan, his head falling back, and I took him deeper. I could feel him throbbing against my tongue, hot and hard and wet from my saliva and his precum. As I slid lower, then back up again, my mouth watering, stretched around his girth, I felt my dick reacting again, even though it hadn't been long since I'd come. I hadn't even been sure I'd be into doing this, but it was messy and dirty and *so* fucking good. I wasn't under any illusions that I was giving him a top-tier blowjob, but I knew he liked what I was doing if his reactions were anything to go by.

Just when I was about to pull off and gasp for breath, his hand came to my hair and tugged. "Gonna come."

He continued to tug on my hair, and my hand went to his cock as I released him from my mouth, stroking him through his climax. Cum hit my face as his cock jerked in my hand, and I swiped my tongue across my lips so I could taste him.

His eyes were so dark and wide. "Your *mouth*. Come here."

I went up, kissing him hard and deep, neither of us caring about the mess we'd made. His arms wrapped around me, and he stroked down my back. "Was that—are you okay?"

Blowing out a heavy breath, I nodded against him. It took me a second to realise that we were *cuddling*. I *never* did this. But here I was, wrapped up in Noah, and I fucking liked it. "Yeah. That was... Fuck, Noah. Believe me, I'm more than okay."

TWENTY-TWO

NOAH

I'd been half convinced that last night had been a dream, but when I woke, feeling the warmth of a body next to me and then opening my eyes to take in the sight of my arm slung across the stomach of my very hot housemate, I couldn't have stopped my grin even if I'd tried.

I reached up, tracing the line shaved into the side of Liam's head with my fingertip.

"Touching me while I'm asleep? Bit creepy."

Startled, I yanked my hand back. Liam's eyes blinked open, and he smiled hesitantly, which turned into a yawn. "Only joking. What's the time?"

"Uh..." Rolling over, I fumbled for my phone. "Ten past nine."

"Shit!" Liam shot upright in bed, suddenly wide awake. "I've got a football match at ten."

He threw himself out of the bed, grabbing his clothes that were still strewn across the floor, and threw them on. When he made it to the door, he paused, then turned back and darted across to the bed.

Swooping down, he planted a hard kiss on my lips. "Bye."

He disappeared out of the door, and shortly afterwards, I heard his own bedroom door slam, followed by the sound of his shower starting up.

I lay back on my bed with a huge smile on my face.

Liam had already left by the time I made my way downstairs. In fact, the house was empty since all my other housemates were on the football team and playing in the match, or so I assumed.

I was just setting myself up on the sofa, happy to have the space to myself, when the doorbell rang. Groaning under my breath, I unfolded my body from my comfortable position and went to answer the door.

"Phew. I was hoping you were here. Forgot my phone." Kian pushed into the house, jogging down the hallway past me. "Wanna come?" he threw over his shoulder as he raced into the kitchen.

"Where?" I shouted after him.

"Football. Preston's playing."

Fuck, no. Then Liam's comment about us not having much in common came back to me, and before I could second-guess myself, I was jamming my feet into my trainers. "Wait for me. Just got to grab a hoodie."

Kian nodded, and I bolted up the stairs, taking a minute to examine my collection of multiple coloured LSU hoodies before throwing on a forest-green one. After grabbing my phone and keys, I rejoined Kian at the front door, and together we jogged across campus to the football pitch, where a few of the players were already warming up.

The stands weren't too busy—according to Kian, the Sunday morning matches never had that many spectators, so there was plenty of room for me. Taking a deep breath, reminding myself that this wasn't going to be like my school experience of football and football players, I flashed my student pass at the steward, and he nodded, letting me into the seating area.

"Here, Ash. Found you someone to even the numbers a bit." Kian flopped into a seat next to a dark-haired guy who I vaguely recalled seeing before.

"Good. Too many ex-Alstone High students here for my taste." The guy grinned, reaching around Kian to shake my hand. "I'm Asher. Levi's boyfriend and former school rival of these three."

I became aware of the two other people sitting with us. A tall guy with rich brown hair gave me a nod, and curled into his side, a pretty, petite girl with a soft smile on her face reached out a hand in greeting. "I'm Raine, and this is Carter."

"Oh, yeah. Hi." I'd seen them with Preston and Kian once or twice, but we'd never been properly introduced. I knew Raine was a student here at LSU, and Carter and Kian attended Alstone College. "Nice to meet you all. I'm Noah. One of Preston's housemates."

Introductions out of the way, I settled back, waiting for the game to begin. This was the first time in my life that I'd ever voluntarily attended a football match, and I still wasn't sure exactly what I was doing here, but it had seemed like a good idea at the time.

"Which team is ours?" I asked unthinkingly, and next to me, Kian snorted.

"Football's really not your thing, is it?"

"You could say that."

BECCA STEELE

"Kian, swap places with me." Asher was suddenly standing, and Kian was sliding into his vacated seat. Asher sat down next to me. "I'm training to be a football coach, so I can tell you everything you need to know."

"Do I need to remind you that I was Alstone High's top striker the year before you became captain at Highnam?" Kian raised a brow at Asher.

Carter leaned over. "And the fact that I was the team captain that year too?"

"And I still know nothing about football except that the point is to score goals." Raine gave me a bright smile, making me laugh.

"Wasn't Preston the top striker that year?" Asher smirked at Kian, who shot him a mock glare.

"Yeah, whatever. I don't mind sharing the glory with my golden boy. Shame you couldn't do the same with your boyfriend."

"We were both captains of our teams, though. *Captains*. What were you?"

Asher's smirk turned into a laugh when Kian elbowed him in the side. He turned back to me, still grinning. "I'll break it down for you, nice and easy. We're supporting LSU —they're the ones in the blue kit. I'm sure you won't have any problem recognising the players. In case you weren't aware, LSU start at one end, and then after half-time, they swap ends. The team they're playing today are Watford uni —they're the ones in red."

"Okay. Thanks." I knew about the swapping ends thing—I wasn't totally clueless about football. I'd been forced to play it on occasion during school P.E. lessons, after all. I'd just never had any interest in it, and still didn't. I leaned back, kicking my legs up to rest on the top of the empty seat in front of me. If my old school friends could see me now...in fact, if my family could see me now...

Tugging my phone from my pocket, I took a photo of my trainers, with the football pitch and players warming up in the background. After sending it to my family group chat, accompanied by the caption "Guess what I'm doing?" I shoved my phone back into my pocket and turned my attention to the pitch.

Perfect timing. The rest of the players were making their way out. I pushed away the sudden uncomfortable feeling that had come over me, reminding myself yet again that this was nothing like my school days. For a start, I knew at least half of the team by now, and they were decent guys. Guys who were becoming my friends.

And then there was *him*. The guy I'd become very, very friendly with just last night. The guy who had kissed me goodbye less than an hour ago. I watched as Liam jogged over to the edge of the pitch and began doing a series of stretches that made my mouth dry.

He glanced up, and I saw him do an actual double take, his eyes widening as he took me in. Unsure of how to react, I gave a lame-as-fuck wave-slash-salute thing. It was the right move because his lips kicked up at the corners, and he gave me a proper salute, which made me laugh.

"You sorted out your shit with him?"

It took me a minute to realise that Kian was addressing me. "Huh?" I tore my gaze away from Liam. "Uh, yeah. We talked." Anything else I said could be incriminating, so I clamped my mouth shut.

He narrowed his eyes, his gaze flicking to Liam, then back to me. A thoughtful expression came over his face. Liam glanced back over at us, like he was making sure I was actually there, and I couldn't stop my grin from reappearing. Kian shook his head with a small, amused, slightly disbelieving smile. "I see."

I didn't even want to know what he was thinking. It was time for a change of subject, and fast. Luck was on my side because suddenly, everyone's attention swung to the pitch, where the teams were lining up.

Watching football had never interested me, but I'd never seen Liam play before. It wasn't even just him—watching Preston, Travis, Ander, Levi, and Damon all playing, people that I knew and lived with or lived next door to, was a new experience, and to my complete shock, I found myself invested in the match. I wanted them to do well. I wanted them to win.

And I had Asher, my personal football commentator next to me, who seemed to have taken it upon himself to narrate the entire match. Most of it went over my head, but I couldn't help the warmth that spread through me as he spoke. This guy I'd only just met, who was training to be a football coach, of all things, had not only welcomed me, but he hadn't made fun of me for knowing nothing. Just the opposite. He seemed to be happy pointing everything out, peppering his commentary with anecdotes about his time as the captain of his school team, playing against the boys from Alstone High.

It was probably good that I had him there to distract me, otherwise my eyes would've been glued to Liam, and I was sure someone would've noticed.

The first half passed surprisingly fast. Neither team had scored, but there had been some close calls. Asher was muttering something about the "incompetent ref" when I stood, stretching out my body after being stuck in the cramped seat for forty-five minutes.

My phone buzzed, and I remembered the message I'd

sent to my family group chat. I opened it up, and yeah, I had a string of replies from my dad, mum, and each of my twin sisters.

Dad: Football? I'll make a Chelsea fan of you yet

Mum: Who are you and what have you done with my son?

Layla: boring

Ami: WHERE ARE THE HOT UNI BOYS

Mum: Ami Louise!

Dad: No boys until you're thirty

Ami: NOAH THEY'RE PICKING ON ME THIS IS ALL YOUR FAULT

Layla: yh its your fault Noah

Dad: Don't you both have homework to do?

Layla: why are you asking us on the group chat when we're in the same room

Mum: Noah, I expect a phone call later to explain this picture

Mum: Have fun *wink emoji*

I groaned under my breath, even though I was smiling. I wanted nothing more than to tell them what had led me to the match today and how much I was starting to like Liam, but I couldn't. Everything between the two of us was so new and fragile and uncertain, I didn't want to risk saying anything until I knew for sure where we stood with each other.

Pocketing my phone again, I took a seat, falling into a surprisingly easy conversation with Kian and Asher about gym exercises to complement running sessions. Before I knew it, the second half was beginning, and although I tried to make sure I followed the game, my gaze kept drifting to Liam. The way he moved, graceful but powerful, his muscles flexing as he ran...it did things to my dick that were way too fucking inappropriate for a public setting.

When the final whistle blew and both Travis and one of the other players had scored, giving LSU a 2-0 win, I huffed out a heavy breath, slumping down in my seat. I'd survived my first full match, and I'd managed to keep my dick under control. Just.

"Are you coming with us?" Kian glanced over at me.

"Where?"

"We're gonna meet the players and get food before me and Carter have to head back to Alstone."

I shook my head. That was a step too far. No matter how friendly everyone was, I didn't think I could be around everyone and act normal if Liam was there. Not only that, but now the game was over, the memories from my school days that I'd been trying to suppress were flooding back in full force.

"I'm—I can't. I need to go. Thanks for inviting me, though."

Straightening my shoulders, I walked away.

TWENTY-THREE

LIAM

Showered and changed, I headed back outside to greet the people who had been watching the match. I scanned the groups milling around, but I didn't see Noah anywhere. I knew I hadn't imagined seeing him earlier.

"Did you see—"

"Noah?" Kian gave me a knowing look, which I ignored. "Yeah. He was here, but he said he had to go."

"I wasn't going to say that. I was going to ask if you'd seen Asher. Levi was looking for him."

"'Course you were, mate." Kian patted me on the back condescendingly. I growled under my breath, which just made him laugh. Fucker.

Not wasting any more time, I jogged away. I wasn't going to stick around for him to take the piss out of me. Whatever was going through his head, he was wrong.

I headed over in the direction of the student union shop, and out of the corner of my eye, I saw a hooded figure on a bench under a tree, fingers wrapped around a coffee cup.

My heart skipped a beat.

Changing direction, I cut diagonally across the grass, coming to a stop next to the bench.

"Hi."

Noah's head flew up, his mouth falling open in shock, but then he quickly recovered, a smile that was almost shy spreading over his gorgeous face. "Hi. I watched you play."

I shoved my hands into my pockets, kicking at the ground with the toe of my trainers. "Yeah. I saw. Decided you liked football?"

He shrugged. "Kian invited me, and I remembered what you said about not sharing interests. So I wanted to come."

"But did you like it?" My lips curved up in amusement as I watched the way he avoided my gaze, clearly trying to avoid answering. "Go on, tell me the truth."

His fingers tapped against his coffee cup. "Hmm. It was alright, I suppose. Not sure you've turned me into a fan of the game, but I couldn't complain about the view."

My heart did that weird skip thing again. Clearing my throat, I glanced in the direction of the path that led to the student car park. "I'm hungry. Have you eaten?"

"I could eat." Climbing to his feet, he finished up his coffee, then dumped the empty cup in the recycling bin by the benches. His shoulder brushed against mine as we set off, and I felt the brief contact through my entire body.

When we reached the edge of campus, I reached out and touched the sleeve of his hoodie before shoving my hands back into my pockets. "I'm glad you came today."

The smile he gave me was wide and bright, his eyes shining as he looked over at me. "Me too."

"I thought you said I was never allowed near your car again," Noah commented as he slid into the passenger seat of my Golf.

"Fuck off." I shot him a grin as I started up the engine. "Want to pick the music?"

"You're letting me pick something? Is it because you don't want me to know about your extensive Justin Bieber collection?"

"If you say one word about being a Belieber, I'm kicking you out of the car."

"Okay, okay." He held his hands up, laughing. "No need to use threats. Your secret's safe with me."

"*Noah.*" As I navigated out of the car park, I couldn't help the smile that spread across my face.

He fiddled with the radio for a minute, connecting his phone to the car stereo, and then a song started playing that I'd never heard before. When he started singing along in a quiet voice, something about catching feelings, I was fucking mesmerised.

"You've got a good voice." I glanced over at him, now we were stuck at traffic lights, and I noticed the flush on his cheeks.

He cleared his throat, and his gaze darted to me, then away again. "Uh, thanks. So where are we going, anyway?"

"Have you been to Crystal Palace Park before?"

When he shook his head, my smile widened. "It's about half an hour away from here. It's...a park."

"I'd never have guessed from the name." He nudged me with his arm. "Is there an actual palace made of crystal?"

"Not quite. There used to be a palace, though." We passed the rest of the journey with me telling him everything I knew about the history of the park. It was fucking weird that I'd not only retained the information from my dad, but that Noah was genuinely interested in what I had to say.

When we were actually walking through the park, a lump formed in my throat that I couldn't seem to dislodge. I tried talking, hoping that I sounded normal, even though inside I was all fucked up.

Why had we come here?

"My dad used to bring me here to see the dinosaurs."

Noah shot me a look that was way too understanding. He didn't even know about my dad, but it seemed like he'd guessed, somehow. "Yeah?" His voice was soft. "What was your favourite dinosaur when you were younger?"

I swallowed hard. "The T. rex, obviously."

"I liked the raptors best. Probably because of *Jurassic Park*." We stopped in front of a sculpture of a megalosaurus, and he stared at it. "This is...big."

"Yeah." Suddenly, I needed to get out of here. "Wanna see the maze?"

Noah didn't miss a beat, instantly lightening the atmosphere. "Is it a-mazing?"

"Shut up."

We headed over to the maze, which seemed to be more or less empty. When we entered it and were cut off from the rest of the world, surrounded by tall hedges on either side, I stopped. "Left or right? You pick."

He grinned at me. "Don't they say to always take a left turn in mazes?"

"If you say so." I shrugged, returning his grin. "Left it is." We began making our way through the maze, and he kept glancing over at me. I wanted to kiss him so fucking badly.

Gripping his arm, I tugged him into a dead end. "Come here."

His eyes darkened, and he immediately came to me, winding his arms around my back and slanting his lips across mine.

This was what I needed.

I lost myself in his kiss. My cock hardened against him, but I didn't do anything about it, just enjoying this moment of kissing him with the sun shining down on us, intercepted by the shadows cast by the maze.

When we broke apart, with swollen lips, both of us trying to catch our breaths, he exhaled a slow, heavy breath. "Do you want to go and find somewhere to sit down?" He pointed in the direction of the exit.

"Yeah. We should leave." His mouth was way too tempting, and someone could come along at any moment.

When we were sitting on the grass, under a tree, I glanced at Noah, who was reclining back on his elbows.

"Like I said earlier, my dad used to bring me here when I was little, when I was into dinosaurs. He died when I was seven."

The only reaction Noah gave me was to roll onto his side, one of his hands finding mine. He stroked his thumb across the back of my hand, and it gave me the courage to continue. "It was an accident at work. He was supposed to be coming to watch my first football match that day. I'd been told I had a place on the school team, and he was so proud." My voice cracked, and I breathed in and out deeply until I'd managed to get myself under control again. "He never got to see me play."

Noah made an agonised noise in the back of his throat, and he quickly glanced around us, then placed a soft kiss to my cheek.

"I'm not telling you this to get sympathy." Fuck, why *was* I saying all this to him? "Tell me about your family."

He stared at me intently, squeezing my hand, before he nodded. "Okay. My family live in the Cotswolds, nearish to Burford, if you know where that is. There's my mum and dad, and then my two sisters, Layla and Ami. They're twins, but they're not identical. They're thirteen. No pets, unless you count the goldfish I used to have."

"Do you have any pictures?"

Surprise crossed his features. "You want to see pictures of my family?"

"Yeah."

"Okay." Releasing my hand, he dug in his pocket for his phone. He leaned in close to me as he began scrolling through the photos, telling me about each image in a low tone. There was a weird feeling inside me. I'd never experienced it before, and I wasn't sure what it was, but it felt a lot like butterflies.

It scared the fuck out of me.

Clearing my throat, I straightened up, shifting away from him. "My mum has a cat called Jasper, and he's practically feral." Thinking about the cat always put me in a bad mood, and it managed to banish that weird feeling I was having from being close to Noah.

"I take it from your face that you don't like the cat?" Amusement danced in Noah's eyes as his lips curved into a grin.

"No. He's evil. It's not funny, so you can stop laughing."

Noah just laughed again, the bastard. "I'll take your word for it." His amusement died away. "Are you close to your mum?"

I picked at the blades of grass beneath my fingers.

"Yeah. Not so much in an affectionate way, like she's not a hugger—"

"Now I know where you get it from," he interrupted me with a teasing smirk that I wanted to kiss off his face. Instead, I shoved at him, making him lose his balance.

I grinned as he stuck his middle finger up at me and then I continued. "But we're close. It was just the two of us for a long time after my dad died. She's got a boyfriend now, though."

Noah read my expression correctly because he didn't ask any more questions. I was happy that my mum was happy; I guess I was just having a hard time getting around the fact that she had someone else to share things with now. It wasn't just the two of us anymore.

"I seem to remember that you promised to buy me lunch. Is there anywhere to eat around here?"

"I did not promise to buy you lunch; I asked if you were hungry. But yeah, okay, let's get food. My treat." Climbing to my feet, I looked down at Noah's smiling face and was struck all over again by how good he looked. So fucking sexy and—

Those butterflies were back, and with them came the panic.

What the fuck was I going to do?

Space to think would've been a good idea, but instead, when we got back from the park, I invited myself into Noah's room, where he introduced me to *Attack on Titan*. I'd never watched anime before, but I found myself invested from the beginning. By the time the sixth episode started, I was reclined on Noah's bed, with one arm slung across his stomach while he traced patterns on my skin with the pads of his fingers. I knew I shouldn't be doing this with him when I didn't know what I wanted, knew I should go back to my room, but I couldn't bring myself to move.

I ended up falling asleep, still holding him.

TWENTY-FOUR

LIAM

My phone buzzed with a text, and my heart skipped a beat when I looked at the notification.

Car Park Wanker: Your lecture finishes at 12 right? Want to get lunch with me?

"Holmes! That better not be a phone in your hand!"

Everyone turned to look at me, and I scowled at my lecturer. He shot me a warning look, and I slumped down in my seat, sliding my phone onto my thigh. I ignored Ander's smirk as I tapped out a quick reply, shielding my screen from view.

Me: OK. Meet outside the library

Noah and I grabbed sandwiches from Pret and ate them as we walked, falling into easy conversation. Or it was easy until he spoke the words that I'd been dreading.

"Liam? I think I...we...what's happening here?" He gestured between us as we turned onto a quiet side street close to the campus.

This boy was giving me all kinds of confusing feelings that I'd never had before. I knew what he was asking me, because it was the same question I'd been asking myself, and it wasn't a conversation I wanted to have without a drink inside me. "Let's get a drink, and we can talk."

"Okay." He glanced around us, then indicated his head to the right. "The George?"

"Yeah, okay."

When we were seated in a corner of the pub's cobbled courtyard area at a small table, pints of cold beer in front of us, I sucked in a breath, attempting to gather my thoughts. *Fuck this.* Draining almost half my pint in one go, I raised my gaze to Noah's. His expression was unreadable.

"What do you mean by 'what's happening here?'" I said finally when the silence stretched into uncomfortable territory.

His gaze lowered, and he picked up the beer mat from the table, flipping it between his fingers. "This. Us. Is this... do you want it to be a thing? Is it just you experimenting, and I'm a convenient option?"

"Uh..." Stalling for time, I drained more of my pint. "I'm...confused."

He blew out a heavy breath, rubbing his hand over his face. "Okay. Listen, I don't wanna push you for answers, and I'm not trying to make you uncomfortable. I just wanted to know where I—where we stand. I guess...I'm confused here too."

I scrubbed my hand across my face. "Yeah, okay. I get that. Look, let me order another pint first." Bringing up the menu on the pub's app on my phone, I placed another order. Fuck, at this rate, I was going to end up drunk in the middle of the afternoon. Noah continued playing with his beer mat, his gaze sliding to mine every so often, his eyes wide and apprehensive, and I knew I couldn't stall any longer. "You're not a convenient option. Don't ever think that. I...I like you. I think you're, you know. Hot. But—" I swallowed hard, knowing that he wasn't going to take this well. "I don't want...I don't think we should be a thing. I'm not ready for that, and I can't make you any promises about if or when I will be, because I don't know. Honestly, Noah, my head's a fucking mess."

His mouth turned down, and his eyes flashed with something that looked a lot like hurt before he quickly masked his expression.

One of the bar staff came out with my second pint. I drained the rest of my first one and immediately started on the second. Noah's pint was mostly untouched, and he sat there, bending the beer mat, his movements jerky.

"Okay. I understand." His voice came out quiet. "I know it's a lot to deal with."

"Can we just...keep it casual? Carry on like we have been and see what happens?" I knew it wasn't fair of me to ask, but I really didn't want to stop doing what we'd been doing.

There was a long, long silence, during which he finally downed his pint, and I couldn't keep my eyes off the long line of his throat as he tipped his head back and swallowed. How did he make one simple action look so fucking erotic?

"You're...I'm...I don't know. How casual are we talking?" he asked cautiously. "Like, friends with benefits, or what?"

"Yeah, friends with benefits, I guess." How could I know what I wanted? Like I'd just said to him, I couldn't make any promises. Until he'd come along, I'd only ever been interested in girls. There was no way I wanted to hurt him, so it was safest to be friends with benefits while I worked out everything else in my head. If it turned out that this was an experimental phase, we wouldn't be bringing anything messy and complicated like feelings into it.

Exhaling a harsh breath, I forced out my final thoughts. "Whatever happens, I want...I need to keep what we're doing quiet from everyone. I don't want there to be any confusion, and I don't want either of us to be answering questions we're not ready for. I'm sorry. I wish I—" Cutting myself off, I shook my head. "I really don't want to hurt you, Noah, and I don't want to make any promises I can't keep."

He bit down on his lip, his brow creasing. "Liam. Okay, look. I—I'm not sure I can do this. It's not you, it's just... You're going to have to give me some time to think about it."

"Yeah, 'course." Fuck. This was such a difficult conversation. Being honest sucked, when I was pretty sure that he wanted more from me than I was prepared to give, and I knew that what I'd just told him wasn't what he wanted to hear.

"I'm sorry I can't give you an answer yet." The words were mumbled into his pint as his shoulders slumped, and I couldn't stand it. Pushing back my chair, I got up and rounded the table. Grabbing his arm, I tugged him to his feet, then pulled him into my arms, speaking low and fierce in his ear.

"Don't you dare say you're sorry. *I'm* the one who's sorry. You've got nothing to be sorry about. Fucking *nothing*, okay?"

Before he could respond, I released him, suddenly conscious that although we were in a quiet corner of the courtyard, there were other people around, and we weren't that far from campus, so there could potentially be people we knew here.

I told myself that I was protecting him from any awkward questions that might come up if anyone saw us, but the sad truth was, I was protecting myself.

TWENTY-FIVE

NOAH

While Liam didn't treat me the same way as Kyle had, and it was obvious that he was attracted to me, I couldn't help wondering if I was an experiment to him. And I could've probably dealt with that, had fun with him with no strings, if my stupid fucking feelings weren't trying to get involved. If I let myself get any deeper, I could end up hurt. Both of us could end up hurt, in fact, and I knew that neither of us wanted that.

So now I had to figure out how to treat him like I didn't want to jump on his cock and to work out whether I wanted to carry on fooling around with him. To do that, I needed time and space away from him.

I wrote myself a set of rules.

Rule one: Don't spend time alone with him

Actually, that was my one and only rule. If I wasn't alone with him, then I couldn't be tempted to do anything.

But fuck, that one rule was a lot harder to follow than I thought it would be when I wanted Liam so badly.

"Tate Modern. Who's up for it? Noah? Liam? Damon?"

177

Travis appeared in the doorway of the lounge with Ander peering over his shoulder.

"Uh, why the fuck would I want to waste my time walking around looking at shit excuses for art?" Damon pulled a face. "Count me out."

Ander rounded Travis' side, stepping into the room. "You're so uncultured. Art is subjective, you know."

"Since when were you into modern art? Or any art, for that matter?" On the sofa across from me, Liam narrowed his eyes in suspicion. "What's going on?"

"Good question, mate. The answer is..." Ander paused dramatically. "Girls."

Travis leaned against the door frame, smirking. "What he's trying to say is that Kira has to go to the Tate to take some photos for her photography coursework, and some of her friends are tagging along."

"Yeah, what he said. Liam? Gotta have my partner in crime." Ander grinned at Liam, and I tried very, very hard to keep a neutral expression on my face.

I could feel Liam's eyes flick to me, but I kept my gaze on Travis and Ander. When I heard Liam agree to go with them, I found myself opening my mouth. "I'll give this one a miss. Thanks for the invite, though." There was no way I wanted to subject myself to girls throwing themselves at Liam or, worse, him throwing himself at girls.

"No." Travis was suddenly standing right in front of me. "You're coming. You're new to London; you haven't been to the Tate Modern before. Right?"

"Uh. No, I haven't. But I'm fine here with Damon," I assured him with a shrug, going for casual.

"You don't like art?" He stared at me, his brows raised. "When you currently reside in a city with over fifteen hundred permanent exhibition spaces? That's just a waste."

"He got that fact from me." Kira appeared next to Travis, and he wrapped his arm around her waist.

"It's not that I don't like art. It's—"

"Noah, come with us. Please." Travis was eyeing me expectantly, and I sighed. It didn't look like he was taking no for an answer.

"Okay. Fine. I'll come."

We'd only been in the gallery for around ten minutes, and I was already regretting my decision to come. I hung back, trying and failing not to notice the way one of Kira's friends was hanging off Liam's arm, giggling and pointing up at one of the exhibits, a circular tower of radios that stretched almost all the way to the ceiling. A shot of pain arrowed through me. I told myself I had no right to feel jealous. But it hurt all the same.

"Travis." I lightly tapped his arm. "I'm going to check out another floor. Meet you later?"

He gave me a brief nod. "Okay, mate. Text me when you're done, and I'll let you know where we are."

As I made my way out of the exhibition space, I saw Liam gently disentangle himself from the girl with a smile that I could tell was fake. He spun around, and his eyes met mine, widening almost imperceptibly, but by then, I was already slipping out of the room.

I walked blindly through the gallery until I reached the escalators and took them all the way down to the lowest level. It was much quieter in this section, with only a few small groups around, and I took a moment to stop, leaning against a concrete wall.

"Fascinating, isn't it?"

"Huh?" I jolted, straightening up to see a guy around my age, maybe a little older, with wavy reddish-brown hair and an easy smile on his face.

"This." He waved a hand around to encompass the space. "Did you know that there used to be a set of huge oil tanks here, back when this was a power station?"

"I had no idea."

He seemed to take that as an invitation to keep talking, launching into an account of the history of the gallery. I found myself caught up in his enthusiasm, a smile curving across my face as I listened to him.

"Noah?"

We both turned at the harshly spoken word that seemed to echo through the huge industrial space we were standing in. My smile was wiped away as I took in Liam standing there, his fists clenched at his sides and his mouth set in a flat line.

I swallowed hard at the dark look on his face, then turned back to the guy who'd been speaking to me. "Uh. My friend's here. I'd better go."

He gave me what I could only be described as a sympathetic smile before walking away and leaving me alone with Liam.

We stood facing one another, our eyes locked. There was so much in Liam's expression that I couldn't read.

"Liam," I whispered.

Fire burned in his eyes as he advanced on me. Without saying a word, he grabbed my wrist, roughly tugging me along, not stopping until we reached a corner, half hidden behind a concrete pillar.

He released his grip on my wrist, his hands going to my shoulders and pressing me back against the wall, crowding into my space.

"Tell me you want this." His voice was a low rasp, his breath hitting my lips.

Did he realise how fucking weak I was for him? I'd just broken my one rule about never being alone with him, and I didn't give a single fuck.

I knew that if I told him no, he'd leave, but everything in me wanted him to stay. Angling my head forward, I brushed my lips across his. "I want this."

My words were swallowed by his mouth covering mine, hard and urgent.

The kiss eventually turned softer, and he sighed against me, his hands sliding from my shoulders, down my arms, to my hands. Threading our fingers together, he rested his forehead against mine, breathing heavily. "Sorry. I know you wanted space to figure things out, but...fuck, Noah. When I saw your face when I was with Kira's friend, I had to come and find you. I wasn't interested in her. Not even a bit. And then I come down here and find you looking cosy with some fit bloke, I just. I couldn't fucking handle it."

"Don't want me but don't want anyone else to have me?" The words came out more sharply than I'd intended.

"I do want you. That's the fucking problem," he muttered. "At the risk of sounding like a cliché, it's not you, it's me."

"It's okay." Rubbing my thumb across the back of his hand, I leaned my head back against the wall. It wasn't okay, not really, but until we worked out this thing between us, we were stuck here in this limbo. "I still can't give you an answer about whether I can do this or not. I'm sorry."

"I told you before, you have nothing to be sorry about. I wish I could just... Everything's so fucked up in my head."

The agony in his voice killed me, and I disentangled one of our hands and cupped the back of his neck. He let his head fall forward to rest on my shoulder, a sound that was somewhere between a sigh and a groan vibrating against my skin.

Swallowing around the lump in my throat, I stroked my fingers across the short hairs at his nape. "We probably shouldn't have kissed, should we?"

"No. Probably not." I felt him press a kiss to my collarbone, and then he raised his head, his gaze soft as he looked into my eyes. "Wanna look around the rest of the gallery with me?"

"Yeah, alright." I fell into step beside him as we started walking back the way we'd come. "Did you know that this used to be a power station? I happen to have learnt several facts about this part of the gallery recently. You might find them interesting."

He laughed, bumping his shoulder against mine, and I smiled.

TWENTY-SIX

NOAH

"We've got to stop doing this."

"Yeah, that's what you said yesterday and the day before." Liam crowded me up against the kitchen counter, nipping at my jaw. His stubble rasped against my skin as he lowered his head to my throat.

"That's what you said too," I reminded him, biting back a moan as his teeth lightly scraped across my Adam's apple.

Logically, I knew that we needed to take a step back and work out what we both wanted, but the more I got to know him, the more I wanted to be around him.

I couldn't resist him.

But I tried. We both did.

Turning away from him, attempting to ignore the erection that was tenting my joggers, I continued shaking frozen curly fries out of the bag onto the oven tray. His hot, hard body pressed up against my back, and his lips skimmed across my shoulder.

"Hmmm. Maybe you're right. We should stop." He slid his arm across my stomach, running his hand down my abs and then lower, until he was rubbing across my cock.

"*Liam.*" I threw my head back against his shoulder, my hips thrusting forwards at the same time he pressed his own erection against my ass. "Fucking cocktease."

"Cocktease? Really?" He removed his hand from my dick, but before I had a chance to protest, he was slipping it inside my joggers, and then his fingers were curling around my hard length.

"Fuck."

Lowering my joggers, his hand began working my dick, making my eyes roll back in my head. He placed his mouth to my ear. "Don't forget to put your fries in the oven."

"Fuck the fries," I mumbled, arching into his touch.

He laughed, but it turned into a moan when I ground myself back against him. Two could play that game.

His strokes sped up, and I knew I wouldn't last much longer. We were playing a dangerous game—we weren't alone in the house, and although there was no one else downstairs at the moment, there was no guarantee we would remain uninterrupted.

"Are you gonna come for me?" He bit down on my ear as he twisted his hand, and my orgasm was ripped from me, sudden and blinding.

"Oh, fuck. Liam." I collapsed back against him.

His mouth moved to my neck. "Fuck. You're so hot."

"Mmm." A shiver ran through me at the press of his lips to my throat. "You are."

"Maybe we should clean up," he murmured when he eventually lifted his head, and I glanced down to see my cum striping the cupboard in front of me.

"So unhygienic." I forced myself to move away from him, pulling up my joggers and grabbing a handful of kitchen towels to clean up with. "This is a food preparation area. What were you thinking?"

"Semen is full of protein, so it technically counts as food." He leaned back against the counter, his eyes dark and heavy-lidded and an amused smile on his lips.

So fucking sexy.

My gaze lowered to his hard cock, clearly visible in his shorts. "You want a hand with that?"

One of his shoulders lifted in a lazy shrug. "If you're offering."

Yeah, I was offering. This wasn't a one-sided relationship—*no*. I derailed that train of thought. This wasn't a relationship at all, as much as I wished it was.

Ignoring the tiny stab of pain, I moved to stand in front of him, leaning forwards and pressing a kiss to his gorgeous lips. Then I got down on my knees, tugging down his shorts and exposing his hardness to me. Precum glistened at the tip, and I couldn't help myself, swiping my tongue across the head of his cock, needing to taste.

He moaned above me, and it spurred me on. Conscious that we weren't actually alone in the house, I sucked down his full length, breathing through my nose, tears filling my eyes as he hit the back of my throat. I gripped his thighs, pulling them towards me, and he got the hint. He began fucking my mouth, his fists clenching and unclenching at his sides as his hips jerked forwards. When he buried his hands in my hair with a low growl, I moaned around his cock.

He gasped. "Fuck...I'm—"

That was the only warning I got. I swallowed around his length as his release went down my throat, keeping my mouth on him until he was spent. When he eventually pulled back, panting, I looked up at him, blinking to clear my blurry vision.

"Was that okay?" My voice was so hoarse after he'd essentially fucked my throat.

"Was that—*Noah*. That was the hottest—"

Footsteps sounded on the stairs, and he went straight into panic mode, yanking up his shorts and diving for the kitchen table. I could see his shoulders rising and falling as he tried to regulate his breaths, his hands holding on to the edge of the table with a white-knuckle grip.

Quickly rising to my feet, I rubbed my hand across my face and turned to my forgotten curly fries.

"What's up?" Travis' voice sounded from behind me. There was silence for a minute, and then when it was clear that Liam wasn't going to answer, I cleared my throat.

"Just cooking dinner."

"Noah? Are you okay?"

As much as I didn't want to, I turned to face Travis, giving him my best attempt at a smile. "Yeah, I'm fine."

He came closer. "Are you sure? Your eyes are watering, and you sound like you have a sore throat."

"Uh, yeah. Maybe I'm coming down with a cold or something," I offered, grimacing.

He frowned. "It can't be freshers' flu—you've been here too long for that. Do you need anything? I've got supplies of most medication in the cupboard."

Giving him a genuine smile, I shook my head. "Thanks for the offer, but I've got it covered."

"If you're sure. But if you need anything, just help yourself."

When I'd nodded in response, he turned his attention to Liam. "Alright, mate?"

"Alright." Liam barely looked up. There was a flush to his cheeks, but the rest of his face had paled, and he still had his death grip on the table.

Travis just shrugged it off, rolling his eyes, and headed over to his food cupboard, pulling out a bag of pasta. I put my now defrosted fries in the oven and took a seat at the table across from Liam.

Okay? I mouthed when he met my eyes.

He shook his head, his gaze shuttered.

We had to stop this. He'd let me know that he was confused, and he only wanted something casual, if anything, and I still wasn't sure if I could handle that. Space was what we both needed.

After today, I'd stay strong and give us both some breathing room.

TWENTY-SEVEN

LIAM

M y thumbs moved over my phone screen as I tapped out a reply to my mum, who'd sent one of her biweekly messages asking for updates on my student life.

> **Me:** Good. Too much coursework though. The lecturers are sadists
>
> **Mum:** Make sure you take time out to enjoy yourself. There'll be plenty of time to live a boring existence of all work and no play when you've got your degree
>
> **Me:** Can't wait *eye-roll emoji* You make it sound so appealing
>
> **Mum:** It won't be all bad. You'll find a nice girl you can come home to every night, and soon enough, you'll be happily married with a family to take care of and to take care of you. Mark my words

I groaned under my breath, guilt—and a tiny bit of annoyance—churning in my stomach. She meant well, and I knew that everything she'd mentioned was all that she and my dad had wanted for me, but right now, with everything that had been happening with Noah, my head was too fucked to even begin to think about anything that might happen in the future.

Me: I have to go now. Love you

Mum: Okay. Love you! Come home for a meal soon. I bet you haven't had anything home cooked since the last time you were here.

Me: That's actually true *laughing emoji* Speak later x

Mum: xx

When I'd shoved my phone back in my pocket, I climbed to my feet and crossed the kitchen to the open back door. Most of my housemates were congregating outside for some reason, despite the cold. Someone had lit a fire in the rusty old firepit that sat in a neglected corner of our yard for 90 percent of the year, and the flames illuminated the faces of my friends.

I felt a sting of disappointment in my chest when I noticed that Noah wasn't there.

"Hey, Liam, grab us some more beers while you're up," Travis called out, raising his hand. Kira was curled up in his lap, both of them covered by a blanket, leaning against the wall. I nodded to acknowledge his request, then turned to head over to the fridge.

I stopped dead. A smile spread across my face, and I couldn't have stopped it even if I'd tried.

"Hi."

Noah's lips curved up, his eyes bright and full of

warmth as he looked at me, and I wanted to kiss him so fucking much. I took an automatic step towards him, needing to close the distance between us, but he took a step back, and then I remembered.

My smile fell, and so did his. Fuck, why was staying away from him so hard?

"Uh." I cleared my throat. "I just came inside to get some beers."

"Want me to help you carry them?" he offered, his voice soft. I nodded, because it meant I got an extra minute of time with him, here in the quiet kitchen, even though our housemates were only a few feet away.

Breaking his gaze, I moved towards the fridge. He came to stand beside me, and I was so aware of him that my entire body was reacting—racing heart and fucking goosebumps included. When I handed him a bottle, our fingers brushed, and both of us jumped at the tiny contact. Noah immediately stepped away, exhaling a shaky breath. For my own sanity and his, I grabbed an armful of beers, and then moved out of his reach so he could get the rest.

Forcing myself to head outside when I wanted to stay took all of my willpower, and the only reason I managed it was because it was clear that he was trying to hold himself back. If he'd given me any indication he wanted something from me, I wouldn't have hesitated. It felt like forever since I'd had my mouth on his addictive lips and my hands on his hot-as-fuck body.

Fuck. I was going to have a dickuation if I didn't think about something else right now. I recited football statistics in my head as I handed out the drinks, until I was calmer. Someone had brought the beanbags outside, and I sank into a free one close to the fire, placing my beer on the ground next to me.

The second I was settled, Noah appeared in the door-way. He glanced around the tiny yard, and I noticed the moment where he realised that the only remaining beanbag was next to mine, because I watched his mouth twist. But he squared his shoulders and headed in my direction.

"Noah!" Travis raised his bottle. "Cheers."

A smile appeared on Noah's face, and he lifted his own bottle. "Cheers."

I attempted to distract myself from Noah by turning to Damon. "Pass me one of those blankets, would you?"

"Here you go." Damon handed me one of the blankets, and I draped it over my outstretched legs. Not that I really needed it—I was warm enough this close to the fire.

"Now we're all assembled, are you gonna tell us the story?" Damon addressed Travis, and everyone's attention turned to him. I raised my brows—I had no clue what story Damon was referring to, but going by the smirk on Travis' face, it was probably going to involve either me or Ander.

"Yeah, okay. So this was our first year at uni. We were clueless freshers, no idea what we were doing. It was our fourth night here, I think, and we'd all been downing shots. Everyone was pretty drunk, and Davis, one of the guys that used to live here, decided it would be a good idea to create a slip 'n slide down the front path of the house."

I groaned. "That night. Why the fuck did we think it was a good idea?"

Travis snorted with laughter. "Blame it on the alcohol. We got all these bin bags and washing-up liquid and set them up. Ander was drinking with us, and he volunteered to go first, trying to show off to the older guys. He only had one foot out of the door when he slipped, skidded all the way down the path, flew out onto the pavement, and smacked straight into a parked car. The car alarm started blaring—this was about two in the morning, and everyone thought it was hilarious. Ander took it all in stride—he somehow managed to climb straight to his feet, even though he could barely stand, and then he took a bow. All of us were shouting and cheering, and the alarm was still blaring."

"You were all *so* drunk. And so loud—I'm surprised no one called the police. Then you wanted to have a go and I told you not to," Kira interjected, shaking her head at Travis, although she was clearly trying not to laugh.

"Yeah, but Liam talked me into it." Travis threw me under the bus. "I wasn't as lucky as Ander. I managed to skid off to the side and mashed my face into the wall. I had the worst black eye for about a week afterwards."

"You'd better not be blaming me for the choices you make under the influence. Drunk you is a twat," I informed him, and he gave me the middle finger.

"Interesting. So the car park incident isn't the only thing you refuse to accept the blame for." Noah's voice sounded beside me, and my head shot around to meet his gaze. A teasing grin was on his lips, and his eyes were sparkling with humour.

"Don't fucking start. Wanker." I lightly shoved at him.

"Bellend." He shoved me back, his grin widening.

Travis laughed. "I got payback anyway. Liam got so wasted that night, he slept through his first lecture the next day, and then when he managed to drag himself onto campus, he ended up in the wrong lecture hall. Sat through...what was it? Forty minutes of a lecture on ancient Greek philosophers before you realised?"

"Don't remind me. I was so confused. I must've still been a bit drunk or something, because how the fuck could I confuse ancient Greek with my marketing module?" I buried my face in my hands while everyone laughed at me.

"Yeah. It took you forty minutes to realise, mate. *Forty minutes.*"

After he was done reminding me of my mistakes, Travis moved on to other stories, and I settled back into my beanbag, swigging from my beer every now and then.

The conversation eventually quietened down. By the time I returned from getting another beer, Damon was deep in discussion with Preston, something about football, and Travis and Kira were more or less falling asleep, wrapped up in each other. That left just me...and Noah.

When I was back in place, I tilted my head to the side, resting it on the beanbag. Noah was already watching me.

"Hi," he said.

"Hi." I ran my gaze over him, watching him shiver under my scrutiny. Wait, was he cold? Reaching out, I pressed my fingertips to the back of his hand. Fuck, he *was* cold. Before I could think it through, I was tugging my black LSU hoodie off. I was warm anyway, and I had a blanket.

"Wear this."

His eyes widened as I thrust my hoodie at him. "Are you—"

"Noah, you're fucking freezing. Put it on."

"Okay." He gave me a smile that was almost shy, and then pulled it over his head. "Thanks." A sigh fell from his lips as he burrowed into the warmth, tugging the sleeves down over his hands.

The sight of him wearing my hoodie...it made me feel things that I'd never felt before.

Things that scared me.

TWENTY-EIGHT

NOAH

Hitting the button to slow the treadmill to a walking pace, I glanced over at where Liam was doing bicep curls in the free weights area in front of the wall of mirrors. He was so tempting—his muscles pumped, his hair damp with sweat, a look of intense concentration on his face as he completed his set of reps. His eyes suddenly snapped to mine, and I flicked my gaze to the windows, hoping he hadn't noticed my blatant perusal. Outside, the rain lashed down, the strong winds sending it crashing against the glass, like it was trying to pound its way through. Normally I liked running in the rain—it was refreshing—but not when it was like this. So instead, I'd subjected myself to forty minutes of torture, watching Liam get hot and sweaty, and my imagination running wild picturing the other ways we could get all hot and sweaty together.

When I'd completed my cool-down, I wiped down the machine, then grabbed my water bottle and headed back into the changing rooms to shower. As I passed the free weights area, I kept my gaze averted from Liam. No point in torturing myself any further. We hadn't done anything since

Travis had almost caught us in the kitchen, and I was back to keeping my distance outside of group situations. I knew it was already too late—whether we entered into a casual arrangement or not, I was falling for him, and the time we did spend together, alongside our friends, only reinforced just how much I liked him as a person. It wasn't purely physical anymore—far from it, in fact, and that was a big problem.

After getting my shower stuff from my locker, I quickly stripped down and wrapped myself in a towel, then made my way to the row of showers, picking the unoccupied stall at the end of the row.

The warm water beating down on me was bliss. I soaped my body up, dunking my head under the spray, and relaxed as the water washed away the sweat from my workout.

It took me a few seconds to recognise the light tapping sound on the shower stall door. My brows pulled together as I stepped out from under the showerhead, flipping the lock and opening the door a crack.

Liam was standing there, his chest bare and a towel wrapped around his waist.

My mouth dropped open.

"Uh. Can I borrow your shower gel? I forgot mine." He was looking everywhere but at me, speaking in a quiet mutter that I could barely make out over the noise of the water pounding on the tiles.

Shower gel? Seriously?

I knew that it was a bad idea, knew that we'd agreed to take a step back while we figured things out, knew that one of us needed to be the one to say no.

But it didn't stop me from opening the door wider.

His eyes raked over my naked body, a flush on his

cheeks that could be attributed to the workout but hadn't been there five seconds earlier.

I licked my lips. "Did you really come here to borrow shower gel?" My voice came out hoarse, and my body was reacting to his proximity in the most obvious way, my dick swelling under his gaze.

He raised his eyes to mine, and his pupils were so fucking wide and dark. "No."

Without saying another word, I opened the door all the way and stepped back under the spray, still holding his gaze. His hands went to the towel, and in one smooth movement, he tugged it off and swung it onto the hook next to mine. Taking a step inside the shower stall, he slowly and deliberately closed and locked the door behind him.

Then he advanced on me.

I couldn't breathe. I was frozen in place, the water raining down on me until his body crashed against mine. Then our mouths were clashing, and his hands were pulling me into him at the same time as he was pushing me back against the tiles. I pressed into him, and he groaned into my mouth, his tongue sliding against mine as I ground my rapidly hardening dick against his.

His lips moved to my neck, and then his teeth were at my throat, scraping across my skin, not quite hard enough to leave a mark, but I wished they would. I wanted him to claim me, to mark me as his.

When his hand moved to my ass, the other still cupping the back of my neck in a hard, possessive grip, all thoughts flew out of my head. Everywhere was hot, hard, and wet, and my senses were on overdrive. I got my hand down between us, circling both of our cocks, and he growled against my throat.

"Fuck, *Noah*."

That was all the incentive I needed to move. I stroked us up and down, the water and the soapy shower gel running down my body easing the friction. He released his grip on my neck, sliding his hand down over my back and onto my ass. His fingers dug into the muscles as he pulled me impossibly closer, panting against my skin.

It was so fucking good.

Without warning, he pulled back and spun me around to face the shower wall. I threw my hands out, planting them on the tiles to balance me as he wrapped one arm around my waist, lining up his hard length with my ass cheeks. His other hand came down to wrap around my erection, and he began sliding his hand up and down my cock with firm, sure strokes that made my breath catch in my throat. My head fell back to his shoulder as I arched into his grip.

He put his mouth to my ear. "Good?"

"So good," I moaned as he did a twisting thing with his hand that sent stars bursting across my vision. He thrust against me, his mouth going back to my neck.

"I wanna mark you up." His low rasp vibrated against my skin. I was so close to the edge already, and his words pushed me over. My cock pulsed in his grip, painting the shower wall with my release. He groaned as he felt me coming in his hand, thrusting against me harder. "Fuck, Noah. *Fuck.*"

Still catching my breath, I pushed off the wall, spinning around, and dropped to my knees on the hard tile floor. Wasting no time, I gripped his thighs for balance and took his cock down my throat.

It wasn't long before he was coming, and I was swallowing around his length, taking everything he had to give. He clapped a hand over his mouth, but I could hear his stifled moans over the noise of the shower, and his body trembled as he came.

Carefully climbing to my feet on legs that were suddenly weak and shaky, I let myself lean back against the wall. He crowded up against me, burying his face in my throat, and I put my arms around him, sliding my hands up and down his back in slow, measured strokes while we both came down from what had just happened between us. The water rained down on us, warm and soothing.

When he raised his head, his gaze was shuttered, and it made my stomach churn. "I need to get properly clean," he said, going for casual, but I wasn't fooled.

"Yeah. Let me just rinse this off, and the shower's all yours." I ducked back under the spray, turning to make sure all the shower gel was rinsed off, then stepped away, leaving the space free for him.

As I unlocked the door, I felt his hand on my arm. I turned to see him watching me with an unreadable expression on his face. "Wait for me. We can walk back together."

"Okay."

I waited for him in the gym lobby. The rain was still lashing down outside, pounding against the pavement, and I shivered, watching people legging it between the shelter of the campus buildings. I was so focused on watching a guy skidding along the path that I jumped when Liam's voice sounded close to my ear.

"Ready to make a run for it?" He gave me a tentative grin.

"Which way should we go?" We could both hear the howling of the wind, and the glass panes in the front of the gym rattled with the force.

Liam's brows pulled together as he contemplated our route, and I was struck all over again by just how gorgeous he was. I wanted—fuck, I wanted him to be mine, more than anything. This wasn't good.

"Library, then Brunel building, then the student union. Then use the cut through by the bike racks. We'll have to run for it after that." He hoisted his gym bag higher on his shoulder and pulled his hood up.

Following his lead, I tugged my own hood up, then gave him a nod. "Let's do this."

The rain and wind hit me, stinging my face like hundreds of tiny needles as we exited the gym and bolted for the shelter of the library. Next to me, Liam was laughing helplessly as the wind blew his hood down and he bore the full brunt of the weather. We made it to the library and paused for a second, crowded in with the other students sheltering from the rain. I glanced at Liam, joining in his laughter as I took in his appearance. His hair was plastered to his head, water running down his face, dripping off his eyelashes and chin.

"Why did I bother with a shower?" His words were whipped away by the wind as we ran for the next building. There must have been something in my face when I met his eyes, gasping for breath under the cover of the Brunel building, because he gave me a cautious look and stepped closer to me, speaking in a low voice. "What happened in the shower... You know that if we keep doing this, it has to stay between us, right? And it needs to be casual. I still don't..." He huffed, screwing up his face. "Fuck. My head's still..."

I swallowed around the sudden, unexpected lump in my throat.

Why hadn't I listened to myself earlier? I shouldn't have opened the shower door to him, and I *definitely* shouldn't have let him in.

If only I could stop myself from wanting more than he

was prepared to give. My stupid fucking feelings were complicating everything.

"Yeah, I know." My traitorous voice cracked, and I cleared my throat, swinging my gaze away from him.

"Noah—"

"Let's go." Without waiting for a reply, I ran for the student union, pulling my hood back and tilting my chin up to the sky. If a stubborn tear fell from my eye, well, he didn't get to see it because it was washed away by the rain.

TWENTY-NINE

LIAM

"Mate!" Travis clapped me on the shoulder, laughing as I jumped a mile at the unexpected contact. He laughed even harder when I swatted at him, jumping out of my reach. "Are you coming to the student union?"

I slid my gaze over to Noah, who was hunched over the dining table with Damon, working on some assignment. We'd somehow managed to keep our distance from each other since that moment in the gym when I'd—fuck, I didn't even know what I'd been thinking when I'd invited myself into his shower. Or my dick had been doing the thinking for me. Fucking bastard.

Returning my gaze to Travis, I nodded. "Yeah, alright. What time?"

"Now?"

"Are we invited?"

My head shot around to see Damon eyeing Travis expectantly.

"If I say no, are you gonna come anyway?" Travis smirked at him, and he grinned.

"Yeah. We're almost done with this project, right, Noah?"

Noah glanced up from the book he'd been studying, his brows pulled together in a frown. His eyes darted to mine, then away instantly, and he cleared his throat. "Uh, yeah. If you want, I can finish this bit, then you can read over it tomorrow. I'm gonna give the student union a miss. Shower and an early night for me, I think."

"Cheers, mate." Damon wasted no time in climbing to his feet. "I owe you."

Noah's gaze returned to his book, and a weird feeling went through me. Fuck my brain, seriously. It couldn't decide if the feeling was relief or disappointment.

The hairs on the back of my neck stood on end. The girl I'd been making casual conversation with sidled closer, her arm brushing against mine, but I barely even noticed, my gaze fixed on the person standing at the end of the bar.

He said he wasn't coming tonight.

Noah's eyes caught mine, and a small smile curved over his lips. In the worst fucking timing ever, the girl I'd been talking to—Jane? Jen? Jan?—slipped her arm around my waist. His smile was instantly wiped away, and the light went out of his eyes. Pushing away from the bar, he stalked away in the opposite direction to me and was swallowed up in the crowd.

"I'm thirsty." The girl pressed closer into me, pouting in a way that I probably would have found amusing if it hadn't caused the guy I was into to get the wrong idea about what was going on here.

Before Noah, I would've found it hot, even—she was the type of girl I'd always gone for.

The thought made me freeze in place. When was the last time a girl had caught my attention?

Since the first time I'd kissed him, even before then, not one single girl had caught my eye. My dick didn't show even the slightest bit of interest in girls anymore.

Fuck. I didn't know what that meant for me, and I knew I'd avoided thinking about it, had buried it deep inside my head, but what I did know was that my dick and my brain were currently in complete agreement.

They wanted Noah. My infuriating, sexy, amazing housemate, who I'd been blowing hot and cold with for way too long.

"I'm thirsty," she repeated when I gave her no response. Giving my empty pint glass a pointed look, she added, "Aren't you? We should get another drink."

Yeah, I was thirsty. But not for anything that was on the menu, and I had the feeling that I'd just fucked up my chances.

But I wasn't a total dick, even if it seemed that way at times, so I bought drinks for her and her quiet friend that had been sitting at a bar stool, playing on her phone while I chatted with the girl. Then I made it clear that I wasn't interested. Okay, what I actually did was pull out my phone and send a text to Ander that read "Want a pint of snakebite?" It was our "save me" code that we'd initiated at the beginning of last year, and he was more than happy to come straight over and start chatting both girls up.

I knew I could rely on him.

That sorted, I needed to find my housemate.

By the time I'd scoured the main bar with no sign of Noah, I was beginning to worry that he'd just gone home. I headed into the second, smaller bar area, which was more of a chill-out zone with big sofas and dim lighting. Pausing by the wall, I nodded at JJ, one of the guys who lived next door at number 1, who had his signature flirty smile on his face. He flashed me a grin before turning his attention back to whoever he was hoping to get lucky with tonight.

Not interested in JJ's latest conquest, I glanced away, scanning the crowd for any sign of Noah.

"Liam!"

Elliot suddenly appeared in my field of vision, blocking my view. Swallowing the sound of annoyance that tried to make its way from my throat, I gave him a tight smile.

"Alright."

He cocked his head, studying me for a second before a smile appeared on his face that I could only describe as sly, and I didn't like it. "Have you seen JJ?"

"Yeah, he's over there." I indicated in JJ's direction without bothering to look, craning my neck to see around Elliot's head, my gaze scanning the crowd again.

"Hmmm. I wouldn't have thought Noah was his type, but now I see them together..."

The rest of his words were lost by the roaring of blood in my ears as a sudden sense of déjà vu hit me. I jerked my body around to face JJ.

Who was definitely, 100 percent, flirting with Noah. And Noah was smiling at him, one of those wide, genuine smiles. *My smiles.*

Like fuck was JJ, with his athletic dancer's body, his casual use of make-up and glitter that somehow only enhanced his striking looks, and his bright, easy-going personality, getting his hands on Noah.

This was a hundred times worse than the day at the gallery when I'd seen Noah talking to that guy. This was JJ, in full-on flirt mode, directing it all at Noah, and Noah...he looked *happy*.

Jealousy and hurt raged through me, burning under my skin.

Noah was *mine*.

As I watched, frozen in place, JJ lifted his hand and placed it on Noah's arm.

That was fucking it.

I pushed past Elliot, storming over to JJ and Noah, and ripped JJ's hand from Noah's arm. Ignoring his sound of outrage and JJ's laughter, I grabbed Noah by the wrist and hauled him out of the room.

There was a small corridor that led down to a storage area, and I made my way towards it. Noah didn't resist, and once I realised that he was staying put, I released my grip on him.

He shot me a savage glare. "What the fuck do you think you're doing?"

"What the fuck do you think *you're* doing?" I gritted my teeth. "*JJ*?"

"Don't be such a fucking hypocrite, Liam." His fists clenched at his sides. "You can't keep dragging me away from people whenever you feel like it. Would you like it if I did it when you were with girls?"

"There are no girls," I hissed.

"No? So I imagined that girl that was all over you earlier then?" His voice was low and angry.

Fuck. No. I yanked at my hair. "That wasn't anything."

He clamped his teeth down on his lip, clearly holding himself back from saying whatever it was he wanted to reply.

I needed to spell it out to him. After a quick glance around to confirm we were alone, I backed him into the wall and planted my hands on the rough surface on either side of him so he was right where I wanted him. "There are no other girls. I'm not fucking interested, okay? I want you. I want you, and I can't tell anyone." It was the closest I'd come to admitting the truth out loud. Yeah, I knew I was acting like a jealous asshole, but seeing him with JJ, when he was *mine*...

The anger disappeared from his gaze. He sighed against me, leaning in to run his nose down the side of my face. "I'm not interested in JJ. Not even a bit. He's not you." He whispered the final words into my neck, then pressed a kiss to my throat.

I shivered, my cock thickening in my jeans as his body pressed against mine. It felt so fucking perfect, so right. "Good," I rasped. "There's no one else I want."

This time when he looked at me, his eyes were burning. "So now you've got me here, what are you going to do with me?" His words came out as challenging, but the shaky exhale against my chest gave him away.

Inclining my head, I put my mouth to his ear, inhaling the citrusy scent of his freshly showered skin.

"I'm going to take you home and make you forget everyone else's name but mine."

THIRTY

LIAM

Preston had been downstairs when we'd arrived back at the house, and it had been torture waiting to get Noah upstairs, where we could be alone. I was fucking starving for him. The second his bedroom door closed behind us, I was on him, my hands everywhere, pulling at his clothes, sliding over the planes of his body, while my mouth met his, over and over, kissing, biting, licking, This fire between us was raging, and when I finally freed him of his jeans and his hard cock pressed against mine with only the thin layers of our underwear between us, I was consumed by him. I needed to have him, to make him mine.

Gripping a handful of his soft hair to pull his head back, I dragged my teeth across his Adam's apple. "Noah." I panted his name against his throat, and he moaned in response. "I need my cock inside you."

"*Yes*," he breathed, gripping my back and angling us towards his bed. We fell in a tangle of limbs, our bodies sliding against each other, hot and hard, until I couldn't take any more.

Lifting myself off him, I went for his bedside drawer,

where I knew the lube was. Grabbing the small bottle and a condom, I threw them onto the bed next to him and crawled back over his body, holding myself up on my hands and knees.

I stared down at him for a second, just taking in how fucking beautiful he was, debauched and dishevelled, staring back up at me through lust-blown pupils. He licked his swollen lips, and I dipped down to kiss him again, my tongue rolling against his. My cock was so hard, it was almost painful, and when he thrust up against me, I pulled back from him, moving to straddle his thighs.

"Fuck, I want you so much." I dragged my gaze down his body, which glistened with a light sheen of sweat, until I got to his underwear. His navy boxer briefs had a damp spot where the head of his cock was tenting the material, and it made my mouth water.

His hand went to my thigh, smoothing across it and making the hairs stand on end, and then he gripped me, his fingertips digging into my leg. "Liam. Do it. Fuck. I need you."

"Yeah." My voice didn't even sound like my own, low and rasping. I tugged down his underwear, and then his erection was free. I wrapped my fingers around his length, stroking up and rubbing my thumb over the sensitive tip. He moaned, one of his hands still digging into my thigh and the other fumbling for the condom and lube. When he had them in his hand, he practically launched them at me, then grabbed a pillow, shoving it under his ass.

"Help put this under me. It'll be easier."

My hands were fucking shaking, and I didn't know why. I was confident with sex even though I'd never done this with a guy before. Maybe it was the way Noah was lying there, so obviously turned on and trusting me with his body.

Maybe it was the fact that I had all these feelings inside me that had never been there before, feelings that seemed to be getting stronger and stronger the more I got to know him.

His hand snaked down between his legs, but I stopped him with a look. "Don't even fucking think about it. This is mine."

He groaned. "Liam. You're—"

"I'm gonna make you feel so good." As I pushed my first lubed-up finger inside of him, slow and careful, my gaze connected with his, and something passed between us, something that I couldn't name but suddenly made what we were doing way more intense than just sex.

"Fuck, Liam," he muttered as I opened him up for me, his hard cock throbbing and leaking precum as one of my fingers brushed against a spot inside him that made him gasp. "I'm ready. Just go slow to start with."

"Okay." Withdrawing my fingers, I rolled on the condom and covered it with a generous amount of lube. Settling into position, I manoeuvred his legs so that they were hooked over my shoulders, and then I was pushing inside his ass, watching his face the whole time to make sure I didn't hurt him. He exhaled a shuddering breath when I was all the way in, buried balls-deep with him so fucking hot and tight around my cock.

I had to hold myself completely still for a minute, counting under my breath so I didn't embarrass myself by coming straight away.

"You okay?" A flash of concern entered Noah's eyes, and it made my stomach flip. This sexy-as-fuck guy was worrying about me when I was the one who'd just impaled him with my cock.

"Yeah. I just don't wanna come too soon. You feel so good." The words came out much softer than I'd planned, and he just gave me this look...I couldn't even describe it, but it was filled with all this affection, directed at me, and the only thing I could do was move his legs from my shoulders and lean down, carefully curving my body over his, then kiss the fuck out of him.

"Liam," he murmured, taking my lower lip gently between his teeth and lightly biting down. My dick was aching, and I could feel his throbbing between us, precum smeared across my skin as well as his. But I was so fucking into this moment, of being inside him, with him exploring my mouth while his hands ran through my hair and then scraped down my back, that I didn't even want to move.

This wasn't fucking. This was next level.

When he released my lip, I dove in for another kiss, sliding my tongue against his, wet and hot and messy, and then it wasn't enough, and I needed to move. Breaking the kiss, I hooked my arms around his thighs for support, angling his legs up and back so I could go deeper. Then I drew my cock almost all the way out of him, as slow as I could, before rolling my hips down again, letting him stretch to accommodate my size. He curled his arms around my neck, the tips of his fingers stroking through my hair as he pulled me closer.

"More. Please."

There was no fucking way I was going to last, not with the way his body was gripping my dick while he begged me to move in that low, throaty tone. I thrust in again slowly, then out, grinding down to get some friction on his cock that was trapped between us.

Noah moaned. "*Fuck*, yes. Like that."

My thrusts became harder, faster, and then we were racing full speed towards the finish, hands and mouths and panted breaths, totally lost in each other. I fucked in and out of him like I couldn't get enough while he moaned my name, gripping me hard enough to leave bruises.

He obliterated every one of my senses, and I came with a shout, burying my face in his neck, my cock throbbing as I emptied my balls into the condom. Somehow, I had one working brain cell remaining, and I got a hand between us, gripping his cock. He came seconds later, pulling me down hard on top of him and trapping my hand between us. I felt his cum hit my skin, his cock pulsing in my grip. When his body went lax, I worked my hand free, smearing his cum across both our torsos in the process, but I didn't think either of us cared.

I let him take my weight and rested on him for a minute with my face still pressed against his throat while he ran his hands up and down my back. When I felt my cock begin to soften, I shifted down his body, slowly withdrawing from him, even though I wanted to stay right where I was. I took care of the condom, then used my T-shirt to wipe us both over. It was enough for now. Sex like we'd just had...my mind had more or less gone blank, and my body just wanted to curl up and sleep, preferably with Noah next to me. It turned out that he was thinking along the same lines because he stared down at me with a lazy, sated smile curving over his lips and held out his arm.

"Come here."

I went to him. We wrapped our bodies around each other's and pulled the duvet over us, and neither of us moved until the morning.

THIRTY-ONE

NOAH

Liam was gone from my bed when I woke up, although the sheets were still warm from his body heat, so he couldn't have been gone for long. I wished he'd stayed, but it wasn't totally unexpected that he'd disappeared. I knew he had lectures this morning, and speaking of—I glanced at my phone—I needed to get a move on myself. I had just over an hour until my first lecture began.

We should talk. Last night had been something that I'd been completely fucking unprepared for, and I wasn't talking about the sex. It was the connection I'd felt with him, something all-consuming that I'd never experienced before. I was falling hard for this boy, and last night had proven that I couldn't stay away from him. Could I be happy with the friends-with-benefits arrangement he'd suggested, knowing it would inevitably lead to heartbreak? Was having him in a small way better than not having him at all? I really didn't want to push him for anything, but at the same time, I needed to find out where I stood with him after last night. If he felt that connection in the way I had— that same, all-consuming feeling—then maybe we had a chance at something more than just being friends who sometimes fooled around in secret.

Or maybe he regretted last night.

Fuck, I really hoped he didn't regret it.

All these thoughts ran through my head as I showered and dressed, then loaded up my bag with my uni stuff. After grabbing a piece of toast from the kitchen, I made my way to my first lecture of the day, which was a financial marketing module. A module that required concentration—which I was currently short on. I took a seat at the back of the lecture hall, then hid behind my laptop screen, hoping I could get away without being noticed. When the lecture began and the first slide flashed up on the screen at the front of the hall, I pulled my phone from my pocket and balanced it on my leg.

Me: Hi. Are you around later?

I got a reply a minute later, and I thumbed open my screen, curving my hand around the phone to hide the glow, not that the lecturer would notice it with me sitting all the way at the back of the room.

Hot Angry Boy: Yeah. Be back home later, last lecture finishes at 4
Me: OK. Come and find me when you're back
Hot Angry Boy: *thumbs up emoji*

Another message notification came through as I was reading Liam's reply, and I swiped it open to find a message from Elliot, asking if I was on campus and wanted to meet up to get lunch with him and a couple of other people from the running club. I replied in the affirmative, then spent the rest of the hour unsuccessfully trying to focus on the lecture. Fuck my brain. I knew I was overthinking everything with Liam, which meant that I was struggling to concentrate on anything else, but that was the way my mind dealt with things.

I spotted Elliot standing outside the Brunel building, and I lifted my hand in greeting, making my way over to him.

He gave me a grin. "Hi. We're meeting the others at the tapas place near the gym. Is that okay?"

"Yeah, sounds good to me." I shifted my bag on my shoulder. "Ready to go?"

"I—shit, wait." He patted his pockets, then began rummaging in his bag. "I think I left my student pass in the lecture hall."

"Let's go and get it, then."

We entered the building, and I followed his lead down a long corridor and up two flights of stairs. When we were close to the top, I heard familiar voices. I froze in place in the stairwell, grabbing the sleeve of Elliot's hoodie to stop him. We both stood, listening.

"...up with you lately? You never want to come out on the pull anymore. If I didn't know better, I'd say you had a secret girlfriend."

That was Ander's voice.

"Fuck off. If I had a girlfriend, you'd know about it."

Liam.

"Yeah? What about a *boy*friend? You've been spending a lot of time with Noah. Decided you prefer your housemate's dick to pussy now?" Ander laughed, and then there was a noise like Liam had shoved him, followed by an exclamation of triumph. "I fucking knew it!"

"Fuck. Off, Ander." Liam's voice was low and angry. "I don't fucking want Noah's dick. I don't want any dick, alright? You're such a fucking bellend sometimes, you know that?"

"Yeah, yeah. Whatever, I'm sorry, alright?" There was a heavy sigh from Ander. "I miss my wingman. Come out tonight?"

Liam sighed heavily. "Okay."

"Yessss. The girls aren't gonna know what hit them."

Dropping my hand from Elliot's arm, I turned away, rubbing my hand across my face. I couldn't listen to any more. Liam didn't owe me anything, but it really fucking hurt to actually hear him deny that he wanted me and to know that he was making plans to go out with Ander tonight with the express purpose of meeting girls...

I swallowed the lump in my throat with difficulty. "El—"

Elliot gave me a look, understanding and empathy and resignation all rolled into one, and I remembered what he'd said about being in love with Ander. *Go*, he mouthed, and I backed away from him, then started down the stairs.

I knew exactly how Elliot felt now, and it meant that I had to end this.

And I would. I told myself it would be easier now, knowing that Liam would be going out with Ander tonight, after he'd spoken with me.

I was getting good at lying to myself.

"Hi."

Warm, strong arms wrapped around my waist from behind, and I smiled, leaning back into Liam.

"Hi."

Then my brain caught up with me, and I twisted around so fast, I almost got whiplash. I pushed back from him, meeting his wide eyes. "I heard you and Ander earlier when I went to meet Elliot."

Fuck. I hadn't even decided if I was going to say anything about it, let alone just blurt it out the second I saw him.

His eyes widened even further, his mouth falling open. Then he dropped his gaze to the floor, shifting back from me. He bit down on his lip, clenching and unclenching his fists. "I...shit, Noah. You weren't supposed to hear that."

"Yeah, I got that part." Folding my arms across my chest, I glared at him, because the alternative was crying, and there was no fucking way that was happening until I got some answers.

"It wasn't...I didn't mean it like that." He finally looked at me, peeking from beneath his lashes, still worrying his lip with his teeth. "Noah. *Please.*"

Inhaling deeply in an attempt to keep my composure, I waited, and he took a step closer, then another, until he was right up against me. He reached up a shaking hand to cup my jaw and leaned in, his soft huff of breath skating across my skin.

My body trembled under his touch, but I stopped myself from reaching out to him, curling my fingers around the edges of the counter behind me.

He opened his mouth to speak, or maybe to kiss me, but he never got a chance. The kitchen door burst open, slamming against the already dented wall, and Travis and Preston appeared in the doorway. Liam jumped back from me as if he'd been burnt, and I collapsed back against the counter.

A sly grin appeared on Travis' face. "What's going on here? Making the moves on Noah, huh, Liam?"

If my eyes hadn't gone straight back to Liam, I would've missed the sheer panic in his gaze that he tried to mask. He managed, more or less...but I could read him much more easily now, and he looked totally lost and scared and so, so miserable.

That look sealed it for me.

I never, ever wanted to see that look on his face again. I liked...no, I loved him enough to take away his pain. Or I'd try my fucking hardest, at least.

I *loved* him?

Fuck. I did. I loved him.

And now, I had to let him go.

It hurt *so much*.

"Are you joking?" I straightened up, twisting my mouth into what I hoped passed for an amused grin. "*Liam?* You've got your wires crossed there, mate. Right, Liam?"

"Yeah," he croaked out. "Are you blind?"

The abject misery in his eyes was tearing me apart, and I took a step forward, then another, and another, until I was between him and Travis and Preston. Gathering the remainder of my strength, I glared at them both. "Leave him alone. It's not funny, alright?"

Travis and Preston exchanged identical startled glances, and then Travis gave a nod, putting his hands up. "Okay. Sorry. I was only joking. We'll leave you to it."

They disappeared out of the kitchen, and I waited until I heard the pointed bang of the lounge door closing before I turned back to Liam.

"You don't have to say anything. But this...thing—" I choked on the word. "—between us needs to stop. I can't do it anymore. I can't be your friend with benefits, or your fuck buddy, or whatever you want to call it. I'm sorry."

"Noah." His eyes glistened. "I can't—"

"It's okay. I understand. I wish more than anything that I could deal with us being a secret. I'd never, ever force you into anything you weren't ready for." The stupid fucking tears were coming, despite my attempts, and I blinked rapidly to keep them at bay. I had to get through this as quickly as I could. As I choked out the rest of the words, the pain in my chest increased, and I was barely able to get them out. "We need to end this before it ends up hurting us both even more than it already has."

A tear caught on his lashes, and he sucked in a shaky breath. "Please. *Please* don't leave me."

Fuck. My heart hurt so much. It took everything in me to force out a reply, my voice cracking as the tears came. "I have to, Liam. We can't...we can't do this anymore."

His whispered reply finished us both.

"You're right. Okay. It's over."

THIRTY-TWO

LIAM

I lay curled up in a ball on my bed, completely fucking miserable. Everything hurt.

I asked him not to leave me. *But he left me.*

My heart was pounding out of my chest. I couldn't speak, couldn't fucking breathe. Panic had overtaken my body.

The second the door closed behind Travis, Noah turned to me, choking out the words that I was dreading. "You don't have to say anything. But this...thing between us needs to stop. I can't do it anymore. I can't be your friend with benefits, or your fuck buddy, or whatever you want to call it. I'm sorry."

No.

My vision grew blurry, and I clenched my fists. What was I supposed to say? How could I make this right? I was no closer to being able to process this thing between us than I had been at the beginning. "Noah. I can't—"

He blinked back tears, and it hurt so fucking much. I'd done that. I'd made him cry.

"It's okay. I understand. I wish more than anything that I could deal with us being a secret. I'd never, ever force you into anything you weren't ready for. We need to end this before it ends up hurting us both even more than it already has."

A tear slipped free. No. It couldn't end like this. He couldn't leave me.

I needed him to stay.

"Please. Please don't leave me," I begged.

More tears fell from his eyes, brimming with pain and sadness, but he didn't bother to wipe them away. "I have to, Liam. We can't...we can't do this anymore."

Seeing that devastated look on his face...it was the only way I managed to force out a whispered reply. "You're right. Okay. It's over."

I blinked back more tears. I'd lost someone else.

Lying here in the dark, lonely and hurting, I could admit the truth that I was afraid to speak out loud. Afraid to even think it. Ever since my dad had gone, my deepest fear was that I'd be abandoned again. That was why I held on to the things I loved so possessively, why I was having a hard time coming to terms with the fact that my mum had a new boyfriend. Rationally, I knew that it made no sense, but it didn't stop it from hurting.

And this time, it was happening because of me. It was 100 percent my fault. Because my head was so screwed up.

Fuck.

I rubbed at my eyes, then pushed myself up and off my bed. Before I could talk myself out of it, I found myself closing my bedroom door behind me and taking the few steps down the hallway to Noah's room. I curved my fingers around the handle and pushed down.

The door was unlocked, and I stepped inside the darkened room.

Noah raised his gaze to mine, his face illuminated by his laptop screen. His eyes were red and swollen, and I *hated* that I'd been the one to cause him this pain.

"Could we...maybe...watch *Attack on Titan*? One last time?" My voice cracked on the words, and I swallowed around the lump in my throat.

He looked at me in silence for a long time, and then finally, he nodded.

I breathed out shakily, padding over to the side of his bed. When I was level with it, he shifted over, making a space for me next to him. He raised his arm in an invitation, and I lay down, wrapping my own arm around him, inhaling his citrusy scent. His body was warm, his chest rising and falling against me as I rested my head against his shoulder.

"I'm sorry," I whispered.

He pressed his lips to the side of my head in a light, fleeting touch. "Me too," came his soft reply, laced with sadness.

My eyes filled with tears again as he tugged his laptop closer and hit Play.

We lay there for a long, long time.

The sky was beginning to lighten when I blinked my eyes open. For a minute, I'd forgotten what had happened, and then everything came rushing back to me.

I hadn't meant to fall asleep here, yet here I was, curled up with Noah, holding him, his legs tangled with mine.

Our last night together.

The pain hit me like a wave.

Turning my head, I found Noah watching me with his wide amber eyes, still so full of misery. Gently disentangling himself from me, he spoke one word through trembling lips.

"Liam."

This hurt so fucking much. "I know."

I forced myself to climb out of his bed.

When I walked out of his bedroom for the final time, he didn't try to stop me.

THIRTY-THREE

NOAH

"Want to run down to the Cutty Sark and back? I know it's longer than our usual route, but it's a nice day, and we can take it easy." Elliot crouched down, adjusting the laces on his trainers while I did some warm-up stretches.

"Yeah, okay." I threw him a smile as wide as I could muster up. The past two weeks since Liam and I had mutually agreed to call it off had dragged by in a haze of numbness. I kept telling myself that it was stupid to be so affected by everything that had happened, when we'd never been together properly, but this fucking idiot, aka me, had gone and fallen in love with him.

It hadn't escaped the attention of our housemates either. They seemed to be tiptoeing around us both. I'd been spending a lot more time in my room, or at the library, or hanging out with friends from my course or the running club.

Elliot saw straight through me, of course. But being the good friend he was, he didn't comment, just lightly squeezed my shoulder as he straightened up.

We set off on our run at a slow and steady pace, our legs easily carrying us through the quiet streets. Sunday mornings were my favourite time to run. London woke up late, relaxing through the weekend, and in the early hours, I had the city to myself. It was something I didn't think I'd ever get used to—passing so many iconic landmarks without tourists thronging around them, but Elliot never batted an eyelid. Sometimes I felt like it would do him good to slow down and appreciate what we had. I knew he'd only applied to LSU because of Ander, but there was so much to appreciate here.

We ran in silence, both of us lost in our own thoughts, until we reached Greenwich and turned left, running past the National Maritime Museum, and eventually ended up in front of the Cutty Sark, next to the Thames. The museum ship loomed over us as we collapsed onto the low wall that ran alongside the path.

Elliot sank down next to me, stretching his legs out in front of him. "That last mile was brutal. I shouldn't have had so much to drink last night."

"Same." I sighed. Last night had been... After two weeks of self-exile from anything social, I'd been forcibly dragged to the student union with Travis, Kira, Preston, and Kian. I was third-wheeling it...or was it fifth-wheeling it? Either way, I was the only single one in the group. They'd done their best to include me, but the last straw had been when I saw both couples holding hands.

It was something so fucking simple, something that they probably took for granted, but it was something that I suddenly wanted more than anything. Someone to hold my hand. To be with me, openly. A boy I could tell people, "Yeah, he's mine."

But after Liam, I wasn't interested in anyone else. I

needed to get over him, and I knew I would eventually, but in the meantime, I had to deal with the knowledge that these feelings wouldn't be going away anytime soon. I was trying my hardest to focus on the fact that I was here at uni to get a degree, not that it helped.

I told myself that everything else had to be secondary to the goal of getting my degree, told myself that I'd get over Liam, but it still hurt so fucking much. Every time Liam and I crossed paths in the house, every time our bodies accidentally came into contact, every time his eyes connected with mine, for that fleeting moment, I was reminded of what we'd had. What we could have had together.

"How are things with Liam?" Elliot voiced the question that I'd been hoping he wouldn't ask.

I thought back to yesterday morning. He'd been keeping me at arm's length anyway, but yesterday, he'd come into the kitchen and actually initiated a conversation with me over breakfast. It had made me feel so happy that he was talking to me that it took me a minute to realise that the way he was speaking to me was different. Our closeness, the easy way we had of talking to each other, was gone, like it had never existed.

"He treats me the same way he treats Damon." Somehow, my words came out sounding more or less normal, but Elliot wasn't fooled.

"Shit, Noah." He stared at me, compassion in his eyes. "You love him, don't you." There wasn't even a question in his voice, only resignation.

I threw my head back, staring up at the soft greys of the sky above me, breathing in the London air that held a hint of salt from the river. Exhaling deeply, I clenched my fists, attempting a semblance of composure, before I finally admitted it.

"Yeah, I do."

Elliot's sharp intake of breath cracked the silence that had fallen between us after my soft admission.

"I'm so fucking sorry."

Yeah. So was I.

THIRTY-FOUR

LIAM

S taring down at my phone screen, not paying any attention to where I was going, I rounded the corner of the gym building and walked straight into someone.

"Shit, sorry." Fumbling with my phone, trying not to drop it, I glanced distractedly at the other figure, then did a double take.

Noah.

He had his hood up, but I could see the ends of his damp hair under the hood, and the citrus scent of his shower gel hit me when I took an involuntary step closer. Fuck, I just wanted to bury my face in his neck and breathe him in.

He eyed me from beneath his lashes, his amber gaze wide and troubled. It made something inside my chest hurt.

"Hi." My voice came out croaky. "Been to the gym?" I mentally rolled my eyes at myself—it was obvious he'd been there, based on the fact that he was carrying his gym bag and was freshly showered.

"Uh. Yeah. How about you?" Shifting from one foot to the other, he lowered his gaze to the ground.

"On my way now."

This conversation was so fucking awkward.

"Oh. Uh...good. See you back at the house." Then he took a step backwards and jogged away before I had a chance to respond.

It was the longest conversation we'd had in days. And it was clear that neither of us knew how to act around each other anymore.

I entered the gym on autopilot, rubbing at my chest, but the ache wouldn't go away.

"Liam? Liam? Hey, man, are you okay?"

"Huh?" My head shot up to see Preston standing next to the pec deck I was sitting on. I must've zoned out for a minute because I didn't even remember taking a seat on the machine.

"Are you okay?" he repeated, eyeing me with concern.

"Yeah, I'm fine."

He sighed, pinching his brow. "If you ever need to talk through anything, I'm here. Kian too."

"Thanks, but I'm fine," I bit out. "Everything's fine."

"Okay. Just...I know you and Noah are both having a hard time," he said carefully. "If you won't talk to me, maybe you should talk to someone else."

I shrugged, staring down at my feet. "There's nothing to talk about."

He sighed again and left me alone.

Everything fucking sucked, and it was all my fault. The only time I felt remotely happy now was when I was playing football, and even then, it wasn't enough.

I couldn't understand it, and I hated this fucking

sadness that I couldn't shake. And the only person I knew who would understand what I was going through was the other person involved in this mess. Not only that, but it was killing me to see him so sad and to know I'd been the one responsible.

Back in my bedroom, I sat on my bed, resting my back against the wall, and stared at my blank laptop screen for a long, long time. My hand shook as I woke up the screen and began typing the words into Google.

The first video loaded. Two guys in their underwear were kissing. One looked a bit like Noah, and my dick immediately paid attention, hardening quickly as I watched the guys move to a bed. I leaned forward, hitting Pause, breathing rapidly. It had to be because the one guy reminded me of Noah.

I scrolled to another video. This one had two guys in what looked like a gym, neither of whom reminded me of anyone I knew. One was lying back on the weights bench, naked, but with a baseball cap on for some reason, and the other was pounding his ass, holding on to the dumbbell bar. It was fast, it was dirty, and it was so fucking hot.

My dick was rock-hard in an instant, watching them. Filthy images of what I could do to Noah on a weights bench played through my mind as I palmed my cock through my joggers.

I forced myself to remove my hand, tapping on the next video. One guy was down on his knees, sucking the other guy off. My dick was really fucking into it, again, and I yanked down my joggers, wrapping my hand around myself with a moan. As the guys on the screen moved to a sofa and began fucking, I gave in and started stroking myself. I was coming, hard, before the clip had even finished playing.

Breathing heavily, I slumped back against the wall.

You're not straight.

Fuck.

How stupid could I be to not realise that? If I thought back on it, after the first couple of kisses with Noah when I was so scared of what was happening, everything between us had seemed so easy and natural and right. I'd never felt that way with a girl, ever. I'd never wanted more than one night. Sex had always been...enjoyable, I guess, something to pass the time, and I was good at it and knew how to make the person I was with feel good, but I'd never felt anything even remotely like I had with Noah. Noah was just...

He was in a completely different league. It was like comparing...fuck, how did I even describe it? Like you'd been eating the cheapest vanilla ice cream from the supermarket for years, and you always thought it tasted okay, but you could take it or leave it. Then one day you tried real, homemade vanilla ice cream, with the little black bits of vanilla in it, so fucking creamy and delicious and full of flavour that you knew you'd never go back to the supermarket ice cream, because it could never even hope to compare.

Before Noah, I'd wondered, deep down, if it was my fear of abandonment that had stopped me from wanting anything more with anyone, but the simple truth was, not one single girl had ever held my interest.

Yet Noah had captured my interest from the second I'd met him, and held it.

Then I'd messed it all up.

What the fuck did I do now? What would my mum's reaction be? Would I disappoint my loved ones for being different? Would I end up losing people I loved?

"Help me," I whispered into the darkness of my room, but there was no one there.

THIRTY-FIVE

LIAM

T hree days had passed since I'd run into Noah outside the gym and then had my revelation in my bedroom. Noah had barely spoken more than a couple of words to me since, not that I blamed him. I knew that we were both keeping our distance from each other until these feelings went away.

Except they weren't going away. Not on my part, anyway.

My head hurt, I couldn't sleep, and my thoughts were going round and round in circles. I couldn't concentrate on anything, and I was so fucking miserable all the time.

I needed to see my mum.

She was still at work when I parked my VW Golf on the driveway of the red-brick semi-detached in Purley, south London, early Friday evening. Using my key, I let myself into the house and made my way straight up to my childhood bedroom. It had been redecorated when I moved out, the blues and blacks I'd preferred as a teenager replaced with soft greys, but my mum had still kept some of my stuff in here. There was a shelf containing my football trophies, and my old

PS4 games were still piled on the bookshelf, with the PS4 itself next to the TV that sat on the desk. The noticeboard still held the ticket I'd kept when I'd gone to see England play Poland in the World Cup qualifiers, and just above it was a printed photo of myself and a group of my school friends, right after we'd finished our final exams and left school for good. On the bedside table was a framed photo of me with my dad on the beach, taken during a summer holiday to St Ives in Cornwall when I was five. He was holding my arms above my head, both of us grinning, with a huge sandcastle in front of us.

A wave of sadness and nostalgia hit me, and I collapsed onto my bed, suddenly exhausted. Fuck, I hadn't realised just how much I'd needed to get away until I was back in the place I'd grown up.

I closed my eyes, and the memories came. Snapshots from my life, flashing through my mind—my dad, my mum, family and friends, and later, girls.

How did Noah fit it into it all? How could I have not realised that there was this part of me, the part that made me want him? I'd always known I was *straight*. I hadn't even considered another way.

Until him.

He'd shown up in my life and completely blindsided me, and everything had changed.

There was a lump in my throat, and it was getting bigger the more I thought about it all. I'd been pushing these feelings back—I'd locked them away, unable to face them, but now they were spilling out of me.

I blinked hard. My vision grew blurry, and the first tear fell, running down my face and soaking into my pillow.

Curling into a ball, I bit down on my lip, trying to stifle the tears, but another fell, and then another.

"Liam?"

I hadn't even heard the footsteps in the hallway or my door opening, but as I lifted my face from where it was buried in the pillow, I saw my mum.

"Oh, *Liam*." She sank down onto the bed, and even though we weren't normally affectionate with each other, she didn't even hesitate to wrap one arm around my back and leaned down to kiss my head like my dad used to do when I was a kid.

I fucking broke.

Right there in my childhood bedroom, with my mum holding me, I cried. Cried like I hadn't done for years.

When I eventually stopped, I swiped my hand across my face and raised my eyes to my mum's. "Sorry," I whispered.

"Liam, no. You have nothing to be sorry about. What's wrong, love?" She smoothed her hand over my hair, concern written all over her face.

"I've—I've messed everything up." My voice cracked. "Everything's gone wrong, and I don't know how to fix it."

Her eyes took on a steely look that I'd seen directed at people on my behalf before. If there was anyone who wronged me in her eyes, she'd go to war. "Tell me everything, and we'll fix it."

"I don't even know where to start."

"The beginning is a good place," she suggested gently.

"O-okay." I cleared my throat. "It started when I was parking my car at uni, and this guy crashed into me..."

The story spilled out of me, everything that happened. Minus the sex details, because that was not the kind of thing I wanted to share with my parent.

At the end, I was so fucking wrung out that I felt like I

could just curl up and sleep for a week. I looked up at my mum, hopeless.

"Liam..." She gave me a sad smile. "It sounds to me like you have very strong feelings for this boy."

"But, Mum, how could I?" My fucking voice cracked again, and fresh tears filled my eyes. "How could I not know that I liked boys until now? What if people look at me differently? What if... Will you still love me if I'm... If I'm g-gay? Bi? Whatever I am? Would Dad still love me if he was here? I—I know he wanted me to settle down with a girl." Fuck, I was crying again now.

Her hand flew to her mouth, and she shook her head violently. "Liam, no. Don't think like that. I will always love you. *Always*," she said fiercely. "You're my son, and I'm so proud of you. I know your dad isn't here anymore, but I was with that man for fourteen years, and I can tell you for a fact that he wouldn't care what your sexual orientation is. We just wanted you to be happy. That's all we ever wanted for you."

"Mum—"

Holding up a hand, she stopped me in my tracks. "I haven't finished yet. I owe you an apology. I know that I've always mentioned you settling down with a girl, and I know I always told you that was what your dad would have wanted. It wasn't... I guess we both just assumed that was what would happen at some point in the future, and I take full responsibility for the part I've played in the struggles you've been going through. I'm so, so sorry. I never meant for you to feel like I wouldn't love you or accept you for who you are. Because I do accept you. You're my son, and I want you to hear me right now. I love you, and I accept you, and that will *never* change."

Fuck. I rubbed my hand across my face, feeling the

wetness from my tears under my palm. My voice came out as a whisper. "I don't think I'm even interested in girls anymore. Nothing ever felt...it's so different with Noah. I just don't know how I couldn't have known before. I don't know what people are going to say or what they'll think of me. I—I'm scared, Mum."

Picking up my hand, she squeezed it gently. "The sad fact is that yes, there will inevitably be some people who look at you differently, but those people aren't worth your time. You have so many people who support you, love. Don't let yourself get dragged down by these negative thoughts. As for not knowing until now, everyone finds out things about themselves all the time. *All* the time. You remember Mr. Peterson, who lives at number 12? He comes to my book club?"

I nodded slowly. "Yeah..."

"Well, he came out just a couple of months ago. He's in his forties, and he was married for almost eighteen years before he got divorced. He fell in love with his best friend sometime after the divorce, and from the sound of it, it came as a shock to both of them. But do you know what? I've never seen him happier in all the time I've known him."

"Oh."

"My point is, everything happens in its own time. Just because you weren't aware of this part of yourself before doesn't mean it didn't exist. Sometimes it doesn't even occur to us to think any differently until something unexpected happens to make us look at things in a new way."

I gave her a wobbly smile. "When did you get so wise?"

"I've always been wise." She smiled properly. "So. What are you going to do about Noah?"

Noah.

It was that exact moment that I realised just how hard and how far I'd fallen.

Fuck. He was *everything*.

And I'd fucked it all up.

My lip trembled, and I clamped down on it, covering my face with my hand. "I think I've ruined the best thing that ever happened to me."

"Nonsense." Her hand patted my back. "From everything you've told me, it sounds as if he's as into you as you are to him. You just need to prove to him that you want to be with him."

A tiny, tentative hope unfurled within my chest. "I don't even know if I can get him to speak to me."

"Of course you can. You just have to show him you're serious." Tapping her fingers on her chin, she pursed her lips. "Maybe you could do a grand romantic gesture; that'll make him listen. Oh! What about skywriting? Or hire a flash mob. Do people still do that?"

"Mum. No."

But she was off on a tangent. "Did you see that proposal on YouTube where the guy got all those people to join in? It was that song by that singer...who was it now? Bruno Mars? 'Marry You.' Yes, that was it."

"Mum! Proposals? Really?" Times like this reminded me just how much I missed my dad. So many of my memories of him were faded around the edges, but for some reason, I remembered clearly how my mum would go off on a tangent at the dinner table when I was little. My dad would humour her for a minute, rolling his eyes good-naturedly, and then steer the conversation in a different direction. We'd all end up laughing, and then afterwards, he'd sneak me some of his dessert when my mum wasn't looking.

She gave a small laugh. "Sorry. No, no proposals. But maybe just a small flash mob?"

"No flash mobs. Ever." A grin tugged at my lips, and it felt so fucking good after the emotional wringer I'd just been through. Pulling myself into a seated position, I hesitated for a second, and then put my arms around her. "Thanks."

Hugging me back immediately, she placed a soft kiss to my head. "I love you, Liam, and I'm always here for you. Your dad would be too."

"Love you too." I sighed. "Wish me luck for when I see Noah again. I have a feeling I'm gonna need it."

THIRTY-SIX

NOAH

I really wasn't in the mood for a party, but I forced myself to go downstairs and be sociable. Hiding out in my room wasn't going to help me get over Liam. These were my uni years—I was supposed to be having fun, enjoying my freedom and all that before I was sucked into the world of full-time work, not pining over someone I couldn't have.

Plus, I'd heard from Travis that Liam had gone to see his mum for the weekend, so I knew I wouldn't run the risk of seeing someone flirting with him, or more. I wasn't ready for that, and the thought of seeing him with someone else made me feel sick inside. It was unbearable, but I knew I'd have to face it one day. At least it wouldn't be today.

Following the sound of the music that was thumping through the house, I headed downstairs and into the crowded kitchen, where I was stopped by a hand on my arm. "Here. Thought you could use this."

Ander shot me a small smile, and I accepted the proffered joint from him with a raised brow. "Why did you think I could use it?" There was no way he could know about me and Liam, surely.

He shrugged with one shoulder, the other arm draped around a girl who was scrolling through her phone, not paying us any attention. "Elliot said you were having a bit of a hard time and I had to be nice." With a surprising amount of insight, he continued. "The first semester at uni is always tough. It's a big change, y'know? It'll get easier, though."

"Thanks." I returned his smile with a hesitant one of my own.

Giving a nod towards my joint, he leaned closer. "Go and smoke that, do a few shots, and find someone to give you a handjob in a dark corner. Or even better, a blowjob. Never fails to improve the mood, take it from me."

Riiight. "Uh. Thanks for the advice." I turned and headed for the fridge, batting away one of the many helium balloons that were floating around the house. After grabbing a can of beer, I made my way to the open kitchen door that led into our tiny backyard, so I could smoke my joint in relative peace.

There was a chill in the air, but the alcohol warmed me as I took a seat on the steps to the left of the doorway. I lit the joint and inhaled. The sweet smokiness surrounded me as I exhaled, and then tipped my can of beer to my lips and let the chilled, bitter liquid slide down my throat.

I was alone in a crowd, but I kind of liked it. Liked that I could be unnoticed, to not have to put on a front and act like everything was okay.

To my left, Damon and two other guys were challenging each other to be the fastest to down their beers. Over to the right, a girl that must've only been five feet tall had pinned a huge guy to the brick wall that surrounded our garden and was attempting to climb him like a tree. In front of me, two girls were vaping, a cloud of sickly sweet blueberry drifting in my direction. Music spilled from the open door, accompanied by the sound of talking and laughter.

I exhaled, long and deep, leaning my head back against the wall behind me.

I was going to be okay. I just had to keep reminding myself.

"Noah? Noah?"

Jerking my head around at the sound of the voice, I saw Elliot peering around the door frame, scanning the backyard.

"Here." I raised my hand to get his attention. His eyes were wide and apprehensive as they swung to mine, and suddenly, the relaxed feeling I thought I'd been starting to get from the joint disappeared.

"What is it?"

He shook his head violently. "It's...you need to come inside. *Now.*"

There was something in his tone that made me sit up and take notice. Climbing to my feet, I raised a brow, but he just shook his head again, pulling my joint and my almost full can of beer out of my hands.

"Noah. Inside."

I turned to the door, and he nudged me with his shoulder since his hands were full, making me stumble for a second until I recovered my balance. My heart rate had kicked up, pounding hard and fast in my chest. Maybe it was the urgency in Elliot's voice, or the look in his eyes, or the sudden certainty I had that once I stepped through that door, everything would change.

Swallowing hard, I straightened my shoulders and went inside.

The kitchen was packed full of bodies, and it took me a

few seconds to see why Elliot had been so insistent that I come inside.

But then I saw *him*.

Our eyes met across the crowded room, and it was like I'd been electrocuted or something. Sparks fizzed through my body, and everything else faded away. All I could see was Liam, his blue eyes fringed by those thick lashes, dark circles underneath indicating that he'd been sleeping just as badly as I had.

His mouth opened, and his lips formed my name.

Noah.

I was helpless to resist.

I went to him.

The crowds parted for me, and I was vaguely aware of curious eyes on us, but I didn't care. Something was happening here; something monumental.

"Hi," I whispered when I was in his space, close enough to touch him. "I didn't think you'd be here."

His tongue darted out to swipe across his lips, and then he swallowed, his Adam's apple bobbing. This close, I could see that the light dusting of stubble on his jaw was more pronounced than usual, and the dark smudges under his eyes were more prominent than I'd first thought. Fuck, I just wanted to wrap my arms around him and hide us both away from the rest of the world.

"N-Noah." His voice cracked, and I realised that his body was trembling. I wanted so badly to touch him, to reassure him that I was here for him, but I didn't know how he'd react.

"Noah," he said again. "I'm...I'm sorry. I'm so fucking sorry. I didn't mean...I needed to get my head straight..." Trailing off, he rubbed his hand across his face, and when he dropped it, the agony in his eyes was too much to bear. I took a step closer, daring to curve my fingers over his wrist. He flinched, his gaze darting down to where I was touching him. Then he took a deep, shuddering breath and closed his eyes.

"I'm... I'm bi."

It felt like the room had gone completely silent, although maybe it was just the people in our immediate radius because I was dimly aware of distant noises. But my whole focus was on the boy in front of me.

Stroking my thumb over the pulse point on his wrist, I stepped even closer so our bodies were almost brushing against each other. "Breathe, Liam. I'm so fucking proud of you."

He gave a small, jerky nod, his pulse pounding under my thumb, and he exhaled shakily again.

"You're going to be okay. I'm here for you. Always." I voiced the words, soft and low, just for him.

His eyes flew open, and they were burning. They fixated on me, and he closed that final bit of distance, his free hand coming up to cup the back of my neck. "I hope you mean that, because I want you. *Only* you, Noah."

My fucking heart lurched at his admission, and I blinked away the sudden moisture in my eyes. "You want me? How?"

He gripped me tightly, his shaking fingers pressing into the sides of my neck. "I want...I want to be with you. Properly. I want you to be my boyfriend." Uncertainty entered his eyes as they searched mine, and he bit down on his lip. "Is...is it too late?"

I shook my head, swallowing around the lump in my throat as our gazes held. Everything I wanted, within reach, if I took this chance.

"It's not too late," I whispered.

As soon as the final word fell from my lips, his mouth was on mine.

"Fuck," he muttered against my lips when we broke apart to catch our breaths. "I missed you."

I buried my face in his neck, sliding my arms around his waist. "I missed you too. So much."

He huffed out a laugh that was filled with relief, wrapping his arms around my body. He was warm against me, his heart rate slowing as we just held each other, standing there in the kitchen while the crowds of people came back to life around us, turning their attention elsewhere.

"Finally got your shit together, Holmes?"

Raising my head, I saw Travis smirking at Liam, who shot him a glare. A wave of protectiveness rolled through me, and I loosened my grip on Liam, twisting in his arms so I could face Travis properly.

"This isn't something to joke about, okay?"

The smirk was instantly wiped from Travis' face, and he gave us both an apologetic smile. "Sorry. Didn't mean anything by it. But you know you two have been completely obvious, right?"

"We have?" I craned my head around to look at Liam. He shrugged and dropped a kiss to the side of my face, his cheeks flushing.

"Yeah. When I say you've been completely obvious, I'm saying I doubt there was anyone on this planet who didn't know there was something going on between you two," Travis informed us, back to smirking again. "You're about as subtle as a sledgehammer, FYI."

Ander sauntered over, sans girl. "Actually, Trav, some of us weren't aware." He rolled his eyes at Travis, then turned to Liam. "I didn't know anything was going on between the two of you. I was joking when I said you wanted Noah's

248

dick, Liam. But you actually do? Wouldn't have guessed it. I s'pose that means I'll be holding interviews for a new wingman now."

"Sorry, mate." Liam didn't sound sorry at all. Angling his head, he pressed his mouth to my ear. "Now I'm gonna do something I've been wanting to do for so long. I'm going to mark you up so everyone knows you're mine."

His mouth dipped lower, and he kissed the spot right beneath my ear. I bit back a whimper and tried to focus on anything but how good it felt to be surrounded by his body heat with his lips on my skin, otherwise I was in serious danger of getting a boner in front of our friends.

But then his mouth was on the side of my neck, all hot, wet suction, and I was gone.

"Bedroom," I tried to say, but it came out as more of a moan. Ignoring the sounds of amusement from our friends, he moved us in the direction of the kitchen door, not releasing his grip on me, marking me again, this time using his teeth.

We somehow made it out of the kitchen and stumbled up the stairs, where he spun me around and shoved me up against the wall, grinding his hard dick into me.

"You're mine," he rasped.

"Yours. And you're mine." I kissed him, hard, and he moaned into my mouth.

Drawing back, he met my gaze through heavy-lidded eyes, dark with lust. "Fucking right I am." He nipped at my lip, then licked over it to ease the sting. "You're gonna fuck me now, and then later, I'm gonna fuck you."

Oh. Yes. I was 100 percent on board with that plan.

THIRTY-SEVEN

LIAM

It had been a risk, coming back tonight, but it had paid off. I hadn't wasted any time after my talk with my mum, heading straight to my car and driving back to campus, stopping only to quickly shower once I was back. The second I was out and changed, I'd texted Elliot to get Noah into the kitchen.

And now I was buzzing. It was a high that I'd never felt before. I felt so fucking light after I'd spoken those words out loud. *I'm bi.*

It had been the scariest moment of my life, walking into that room and not knowing what the consequences of my actions would be, but the second I'd locked eyes on Noah, I knew that whatever happened, it was all worth it.

And now I was more turned on than I'd ever been in my life, about to get dicked down by my incredibly hot boyfriend, and everyone knew we were together. No more hiding. I'd claimed him as mine in front of all our friends, and now I could kiss him anytime I wanted. And more.

He moaned, arching his body into mine as we ground our dicks together, tugging at my T-shirt to lift it over my head. We were still in the hallway, but it didn't seem like he cared.

"Come into the bedroom." I wrestled his T-shirt off, then pressed into him, relishing the feel of his gorgeous body against mine. His hand went to his jeans, unbuttoning them, and then he shoved them down and kicked them off, uncaring that he was leaving them strewn across the hallway floor.

I didn't care either. I shoved my own jeans down and left them with his before placing a hand to his chest and pushing him in the direction of my bedroom. I could feel his laughter against my palm, but he complied, letting me push him inside.

The second the door slammed shut, I released my grip on him for the few seconds it took us both to swipe our socks from our feet, and then I was shoving him backwards onto my bed. Our mouths met in a hot, wet, messy kiss, and I poured everything I was feeling into it.

"Liam."

When I opened my eyes, Noah was staring up at me through blown pupils. I nipped at his bottom lip, and he smiled. That smile did things to my insides—butterflies, stomach flipping, the whole works. I was so fucking gone for him.

"Is this really happening?"

I pressed another kiss to his addictive lips. "Yeah, it's happening. You and me. We're happening."

"Mmm. I'm about to have sex with my boyfriend." His smile widened, but it was instantly wiped away when I ground my dripping cock against his. He groaned, arching up into me. "Fuuuck. Don't stop."

"I won't." Drawing him into another kiss, I rolled my hips against his, his cock sliding thick and heavy against mine. It felt so fucking good, it took everything in me to pull back, leaving him panting beneath me.

"You said you wouldn't stop."

"I know. I need...we need to get me ready, otherwise I'm not gonna last."

He reached up to lightly grip my jaw, brushing his thumb across my stubble. "Are you sure you want to do it this way round?"

"Yeah." I rolled off him, onto my back. "Fucking you was the best sex I'd ever had in my life, hands down, and now I want to try it this way. I want to feel your dick inside me."

"Liam," he groaned, his hand pressing down on his cock as he threw his head back against the pillow. His teal boxer briefs were damp with precum, and it made my mouth water. Fuck it, I could wait. I needed my mouth around his cock, right now.

I moved onto my knees, shifting down the bed until my head was level with the tent in his underwear. Closing my mouth over the head of his cock through the soft fabric, I licked over his hardness, hearing him gasp above me. I glanced up at him, shooting him a smirk as I eased down his underwear, freeing his erection.

The second his underwear was out of the way, I licked a long stripe up his cock as my hand went to his balls. His hands came down to my hair, and when I swirled my tongue around the head, his grip tightened. I took him deeper, my fingers sliding over his balls and then pressing against his taint. There was a moan, followed by a sharp yank on my hair, and I reluctantly released him.

"If you want to experience anal, then you need to stop, because I'm *this* close to coming." His chest rose and fell with his rapid breaths, and there was barely any amber left in his gaze, his pupils were so huge and dark.

"Fine." I dragged my hand up his length and ran my thumb over his slit, gathering the moisture at the tip. When I licked around my thumb, then took it into my mouth, tasting his precum, he gave a filthy low moan that made my dick throb.

"I've never...you're so..." He trailed off helplessly, throwing his hand over his face. "There's no one like you."

"In a good way?" I crawled up his body, caging him in with my forearms.

He lowered his hand from his face, and his eyes met mine. "The best way."

Then he surged up to kiss me. His arms came around me, and he rolled us so I was on my back again. Sliding down my body, placing kisses all over me, dragging his teeth across my skin, he drove me completely wild before he was anywhere near my dick. When he finally tugged down my underwear, he sat back on his knees, his heated gaze burning me all over as he looked his fill.

"You are so fucking sexy."

The way he spoke so hoarsely, staring at me like that...it was almost too much. No one had ever looked at me that way before. I'd fallen so fucking hard for him, and maybe, just maybe, he'd fallen just as hard with me.

"You..." I licked my suddenly dry lips, trying again. "You are too. You're beautiful."

Something flashed in his eyes, something so soft and fragile, and I wanted more of it, but then heat flared again as he took my cock in his hand and began to stroke.

His other hand went to my balls, then dipped lower, slowly rubbing over my taint.

"Mmm. Noah. So good." My eyes rolled back as he

tortured me with slow movements, bringing me close to the edge but never letting me get near enough to tip over.

He paused in his movements to grab the lube and condom I'd left out on the side earlier, hoping with everything I had that tonight would go well enough for us to get to this point. The corners of his lips kicked up in amusement as he took in the supplies waiting there, and he bent down to give me a swift kiss, smiling against my lips. He kissed me once more, then pulled back. "Fuck, Liam. Look at you." His hand trailed across my pecs, his thumbs lightly rubbing over my nipples, and I groaned. It felt so good, and the way he was looking at me right now, with that molten gaze...I was so fucking hard, and I needed him.

"Noah. I want you."

He lowered his head, brushing his lips against mine. "You're going to have me. I think it'll be more comfortable for you if you turn over."

"Okay." When he moved off me, I turned onto my stomach, and he shifted me into position so I was resting my weight on spread knees and forearms with my head on my pillow. There was the sound of a cap popping off, and then a cool, slippery finger was brushing across my hole.

I couldn't help it—I tensed up, gritting my teeth, sudden nerves overtaking me.

"Hey." His body curled over mine, and he placed his mouth close to my ear. "If you don't like this, if you want to stop at any point, you just have to say, and I'll stop straight away."

"Okay," I whispered, blowing out a shaky breath.

He pressed a kiss to the back of my neck. "Even if we do this and you decide you never want to do it again, it's okay, Liam. I want you. The hows and whys aren't important to me, as long as I have you."

Something inside me relaxed at his words. "You have me, no matter what. I...I want to do this. I'm just...y'know, your dick isn't exactly small, and I've never done this before."

"I'll take care of you. Just relax and breathe, and anytime you want me to slow down or stop, just say." Pressing another kiss to the back of my neck, he began to circle his finger around my hole in a massaging movement, swiping down over my taint, then back again, until my fears were forgotten, and I was pushing back against him.

"Touch your cock," he murmured, low and sexy, and I shifted my body, getting a hand underneath myself to wrap around my cock. As a groan escaped me, he pushed one finger inside me, all the way to the knuckle. I gasped, clenching around his finger, but after the initial shock, I realised it hadn't hurt.

"More," I commanded, pushing back again.

"Liam. You're going to kill me," he moaned, easing a second lubed finger inside my ass. He stayed still for a minute, letting me get used to the sensation, placing kisses down my spine while I stroked my cock, keeping my grip loose so I didn't lose it before he even got inside me.

After a minute, he began to move his fingers, circling and scissoring, stretching me. There was a slight burn that soon disappeared until he added a third finger. But he seemed to be able to read me perfectly because the next moment, I felt more cool lube added, and then as his fingers began moving again, it was a slow, easy glide.

"Breathe," he reminded me. "How're you doing?"

"Good. I—" My words were cut off by a choked gasp as he hit a spot inside me that felt so fucking good. "Oh my— fuck. Do that again."

He didn't reply, just circled his fingers again and

brushed that same spot. I clamped my teeth down on my lip to stop myself from crying out. My cock throbbed in my grip, precum leaking from the tip, and I knew that it would be all over any minute now.

"Noah. Get your dick inside me. Now."

The urgency in my voice must've been obvious because his fingers immediately stilled, and then he carefully withdrew them. I heard the sound of a packet tearing, and then the blunt head of his cock was at my entrance. "Breathe," he said again, low and husky, and then he pressed inside me, slow and steady, until he was all the way in.

So. Full.

I swallowed hard, trying to regulate my breathing, letting myself adjust to the feel of the full length of his cock inside me, stretching me out.

"Okay?" He curled over me again, his front all along my back, and I twisted my head to meet his gaze.

"Yeah. I'm okay."

A small smile curved across his lips. "You feel so good."

I flexed my ass, and he groaned, which made me smile. "Come here and kiss me."

He angled his head, and his lips met mine, hot and wet, his tongue stroking into my mouth as we deepened the kiss. "I'm gonna move now," he whispered when we broke apart.

Giving him a quick nod to let him know I was okay, I dropped my head back to the pillow, fisting my cock as he withdrew slowly until only the tip of his cock was inside me, then slid back in again. He kept up the slow pace until I was pushing back, moaning into the pillow, and then he began to work his hips harder, faster, thrusting in and out of me. He adjusted the angle slightly, and then his cock was pressing against that spot inside me that felt so fucking good.

My eyes rolled back, and my breath caught in my

throat. Panting, I pushed back against him. "Feels so— I'm gonna come." My hand moved faster over my dick, and then I was falling over the edge, hot cum covering my hand and the sheets. Noah moaned, and I felt him shake against my body moments later, his cock pulsing inside me as he came. He collapsed down on my back with a long groan, his body hot and sweaty against mine.

It took a long time for my breathing to go back to normal. My head was spinning, and not only because of what we'd just done. The sex had reaffirmed just how much I wanted him and how serious I was about him.

There was no way I was ever letting him go.

After softly kissing a spot just behind my ear, he withdrew from me. I was vaguely aware of the soreness that I knew would probably be worse later, but at the moment, I was too high on endorphins to care. Rolling onto my back, away from the wet patch, I watched him tie off the condom and launch it into the bin, then disappear into the bathroom.

When he returned, naked, flushed, and very, very gorgeous, he was holding a towel and a glass of water.

"Here." He handed me the water, then used the towel to carefully clean me up. "How was that?"

I gave him a sleepy, sated smile. "So good. You?"

Clambering into the bed next to me and arranging the sheets so we were both lying on a clean part of the bed, he laid his head on my chest. "Mmm. The best."

Sliding my arm around him, I pulled him closer, dropping a kiss to his head. "Noah? Do you prefer it that way? Or do you prefer me fucking you?"

He shrugged against me. "I'm vers, but like I said earlier, I want you any way I can have you. If you prefer one way over another, I'm fine with it."

I stroked my fingers down his back, smiling as he shivered beneath my touch, curling his arm around my torso. "I think we need more research. A lot more research. Every way, in every position."

"Mmm." A yawn overtook him. "I like the sound of that."

"I know I said I was going to fuck you after you fucked me, but let's nap now, yeah?" Pulling the covers over us, I met his gaze as he looked up at me through heavy-lidded eyes. He nodded, letting his eyes fall closed, and he lowered his head to press his face against my neck.

It didn't take long for his breathing to even out, soft huffs against my skin.

I'd missed sleeping with him *so much*.

I lay there for a while, just holding him, thinking about how much my life had changed in such a short time, and then sleep took me too.

THIRTY-EIGHT

NOAH

Something was pressed against my ass. Something hard, and—oh. A smile crossed my face, and I pressed backwards.

"Mmm. Morning." Liam's sleepy rumble sounded close to my ear, his hand running over my abs. "I could get used to this."

"Me too." I stretched, still deliciously sore from last night. We'd napped for around an hour, showered to wake ourselves up, and then like he'd promised, he'd fucked me. Right there in the shower. Then we'd collapsed into bed, cued up an episode of *Attack on Titan*, and we'd fallen asleep together watching it.

Glancing over at my phone, I saw it was eight-fifteen. Still early, and it was Saturday. No one else would be up yet, I could guarantee. Everyone would still be crashed out from last night's party.

Which meant that Liam and I ran no risk of being disturbed, and going by the way he was now grinding his cock into me, he had one thing on his mind. The same thing I did.

But first...I twisted around, giving him a closed-mouth kiss. He smiled, all soft and sleepy, and it did things to me. I loved this boy. It was too soon to tell him, I knew, but there was no doubt in my mind.

I can't believe I have the boy of my dreams in my bed.

"Technically, it's my bed, but whatever."

"Huh?" My eyes widened, and then I felt my cheeks heating as I realised I'd spoken my thoughts aloud. "Ugh," I groaned. "That was supposed to stay in my head."

He huffed out a laugh, leaning forward to kiss the tip of my nose. "I can't believe I have you here either." My helpless smile probably gave away too many of my feelings, but he just pulled me closer, wrapping his arms around me and placing a soft kiss to my cheek. "How sore are you?"

Hugging him back tightly, I murmured, "Not too sore. But I'm going to use your bathroom first." Forcing myself to leave the warmth of his bed, I padded into his en suite, and when I returned, freshened up with the taste of mint in my mouth rather than the gross morning taste, he followed suit.

Finally, we were back in bed, under the covers, trading lazy kisses while our hands explored each other. The morning sun, diffused by his window blinds, cast a soft, dim light across the bed, and everything was slow and relaxed and like nothing I'd ever experienced before.

It was like we were in our own world, just the two of us. The prep seemed to take no time at all, and when he pulled me upright and onto my knees, situating himself on his own knees behind me, my back to his chest, we moved in perfect synchronicity, his cock sliding inside me with ease. I rested my head back on his shoulder as he kissed down my neck, palming my cock with slow, even strokes. Then we began to move, and it was fucking sublime.

His grip grew firmer, faster.

"Liam. Liam. *Liam.*" All I could do was pant his name as I came so hard that I saw stars. His teeth clamped down on my throat, and he groaned into my neck long and low, thrusting up into me as his own climax hit him.

"*Noah*. Fuck. I lo—" He buried his face in my shoulder, cutting his words off, but my heart raced, imagining what he might have said. But there was no way he'd be feeling that, not yet. It was enough that he'd chosen me, made a public commitment to me when he asked me to be his boyfriend.

Everything else would come in time.

A couple of hours later, we were downstairs in the kitchen, still alone. Around us, debris from the party littered the surfaces—bottles, cans, spilled drinks, but both of us ignored the mess. I reached up to the cupboard for mugs, and Liam came up behind me, his arms sliding around my waist as he kissed the back of my neck. I shivered at his touch, carefully placing the mugs down before I turned in his arms.

He looked at me, his blue eyes wide and serious, and angled his head forwards, his lips brushing against mine. "All I want to do is kiss you. I'm fucking addicted to your mouth."

"You can kiss me anytime you want," I whispered, closing the millimetres of distance between us, losing myself in the hot, slow slide of his mouth against mine.

"Is this what we have to look forward to now?"

The loud voice from behind Liam had us jumping apart. Travis stood in the doorway, smirking at us.

"Yeah, it is." Liam tugged me back to him, planting an exaggerated kiss on my lips.

Travis just rolled his eyes, strolling past us to put the

kettle on. "I'm sure I wasn't this sickeningly sweet when I first got together with Kira. Thanks," he added as I passed him two mugs, assuming that Kira had stayed over after the party. He added tea bags, then propped himself up against the counter. "Seriously, though. It was obvious you were into each other, and I'm glad you managed to sort all your shit out."

"Thanks." I shot him a smile as I added a tea bag to my own mug. "Liam? Tea? Coffee?"

"Coffee, but I can make it." Liam squeezed my hand before moving to place his mug under the nozzle of the coffee machine. "By the way, Trav, you and Kira were much worse, just for the record."

"Nah, I think you're mistaken. You two are nauseating. Can't let go of each other for one second."

"We're not touching each other right now," Liam pointed out. He shot me a teasing grin, and then blew me a kiss. I laughed, stepping over to him and placing a quick kiss to his smiling mouth, before returning to my position in front of the kettle.

"Thanks for proving my point, Noah." Travis saluted me, smirking as Liam faced him and threw his middle finger up.

"Always happy to help. Although I'm obligated to side with Liam, since he's my boyfriend."

At the word "boyfriend," Liam glanced over at me, and he gave me a soft look that made me melt. I still couldn't believe that he was mine, but he was, and the way he was showing it so openly in front of our friends...this was the happiest I'd ever been. And I was pretty sure he was happy too, judging by the smile that seemed to be permanently on his face today.

Then a sudden thought struck me. "My boyfriend is a footballer. How the fuck did I end up with a *footballer*?"

Liam and Travis both started laughing, and Liam's grin turned evil. "As part of your boyfriend privileges, you get to come to allll my matches."

"No!" I buried my face in my hands with a loud groan. "Is it too late to back out? Someone save me from this torture."

"Too late. You're stuck with me now."

"I guess there are some upsides to being with you." I shamelessly raked my gaze over him, and his eyes darkened, his tongue darting out to slide over his lips as he stared right back at me.

"No eye fucking in the kitchen. House rule," Travis called from the fridge, where he was rummaging through the shelves. "Moving on to more important topics—does anyone have any food? I'm out of eggs, and there's no bacon."

"Nah, I used the last of my eggs on Thursday. Want to order?" Liam suggested. He grinned when my stomach rumbled as if on cue.

Travis was already pulling out his phone. "Maccy D's? I don't know how many people stayed over, but if I order enough McMuffins and hash browns for twenty of us, they'll get eaten, right?"

As I poured boiling water from the kettle into the three mugs, Liam moved back to stand beside me, curling his arm around my waist. "Yeah. Do it."

And he did, and it was the best morning I'd had since I'd moved here. More people gradually began to wake up, congregating in the kitchen, where we all feasted on McDonald's breakfast, washed down with huge mugs of tea and coffee.

After that, all the housemates gathered together to tackle the clean-up, with Liam stealing kisses from me whenever he could as we worked to get the house back into some kind of order.

When we were done and everyone else had left other than Kian, who was staying over until Sunday, we collapsed on the sofas in the lounge. Liam was thumbing at his phone, and I leaned my head towards his, curious.

When he saw me looking, he shielded his phone with his hand. "Eyes off my phone." I raised a brow, staring at him until he elaborated, amusement dancing in his eyes. "I'm planning something for us, okay? So keep your eyes to yourself, or it'll ruin the surprise."

A wide smile overtook my face. "Okay."

Whatever it was, I couldn't wait.

THIRTY-NINE

NOAH

"Noah. Wake up."

I groaned, burying my face in the pillow.

"Noah." A hand was lightly shaking my arm. "Come on. We'll be late."

At those words, I blinked my eyes open, and Liam eventually came into focus, his head propped on his arm as he watched me.

"Hi," I rasped, my throat dry.

"Morning. Time to get up. We can't miss our time slot."

"Time slot?"

"You'll see."

London was so quiet at early o'clock on a Sunday morning. It was still dark outside as we headed away from the campus, towards London Bridge. I tugged the sleeves of my hoodie down over my hands, the chill in the air making my fingers turn to icicles.

"Cold?" Liam shot me a sideways glance.

"A bit."

He moved closer, and then suddenly, his fingers were sliding between mine. "Is that better?"

I could only nod. It was something so fucking simple, but he was holding my hand, in public, and he'd been the one to initiate it.

"Good." He rubbed his thumb across my knuckle, giving me a soft smile.

We fell silent as we walked across the bridge, hand in hand. His palm was so warm against mine, and I didn't think I'd ever get enough of this closeness.

After we'd passed Monument tube station and crossed the road, I glanced around me. I didn't know this part of London well, and I couldn't work out where Liam was taking me.

"Where are we going?" I doubted he'd tell me, but it was worth a try.

"You'll see," was all he said.

A few minutes later, we stopped in front of the entrance to a towering skyscraper with plants covering the outer surface of the bottom part. He tugged me towards the automatic doors, and when we entered, he showed something on his phone to the person behind the reception desk, who directed us towards a lift. There were a few other people around, looking as sleepy as I felt.

Eventually the lift doors opened again, and we stepped out into a huge space with towering glass walls surrounding us, showcasing a 360-degree view of London, stretching away as far as the eye could see. The sky was just beginning to lighten, the sun peeking over the horizon, sparkling on the river and the buildings beneath us, and the sight took my breath away.

"Wow," I breathed. "This is amazing."

"You like it?"

Liam's tone had me turning to look at him. He was eyeing me uncertainly, his teeth clamped down on his lip.

"I love it."

His face cleared, and he smiled. "This is the Sky Garden. I always thought I wanted to bring someone here one day, but there's never been anyone I wanted to share it with." He stepped closer. "Until you."

Our lips met, right there, out in the open. We were just two boys kissing each other, with no fears, nothing to hide. Just another couple who were so into each other that we couldn't help but show it.

"Show me the rest of it," I said when he released me, his fingers again slipping between mine.

He led me up the steps at the side of the three storeys of indoor landscaped gardens, weaving through the greenery that was carefully placed throughout the huge space, across the top, and back down the other side, where we joined the other people watching the sunrise. When he pulled out his phone, turned us around, and threw his arm around me, I couldn't stop my smile even if I'd tried. He took a few selfies of us with the sun in the background and immediately posted one to his social media. I forwarded the link to my family group chat with the caption "me and my boyfriend," then turned my phone off so I could focus on him.

When our time was up and we'd fuelled up on coffee from the Sky Garden cafe, we wandered back down to the river, our hands still clasped.

"What made you decide to, uh, come out?" The question that had been at the back of my mind ever since his confession in the kitchen spilled from my lips.

He came to a standstill next to the stone wall that bordered the riverside path. His gaze distant, he stared across the Thames. Eventually, he spoke. "I was fucking miserable without you, Noah. Really, really miserable. I don't...I didn't realise how hard it would be. How much I— I'd miss you. I had to get away, because it was killing me." His voice cracked, and he paused, clearing his throat before he continued. "I went to see my mum. I was telling her about you, and it just hit me all at once."

I moved closer to him. "I missed you too, Liam. So much. It was so hard without you."

When he turned to look at me, his expression was anguished. "It was my fault. I hurt you, and I'm so fucking sorry."

"No." Shaking my head, I wrapped my arms around him. "All that's in the past. You don't have to be sorry for anything. We're together now, and that's what matters."

He breathed a deep, shuddering breath, dipping his head to my neck as he hugged me to him. "Yeah. I'm never letting you go again." When he raised his head, he met my gaze. "You're *mine*. I'll tell the whole fucking world if I have to. Even if it means I have to hire a skywriter or a fucking flash mob."

A smile tugged at my lips, which he returned. The three words were on the tip of my tongue, and I swallowed them down with an effort. Now wasn't the time.

"So to answer your question, I guess you were the one who made me realise that I was into guys, and when I finally got my head around it all, I didn't want to hide it anymore. I wanted to be with you as your boyfriend." He gave me another soft smile.

"I'm so glad you did."

The sun's rays made the water next to us sparkle, catching my eye as he gripped my chin. "Me too. Noah, listen." The seriousness in his tone had me giving him my full attention, and as I looked into his beautiful blue eyes, my stomach flipped. His warm breath hit my lips as he spoke so quietly, just for me. "I know it's way too soon for this, but...fuck it. I need to tell you."

"Tell me what?" My voice shook.

"That I...that I love you."

I stared at him, my mouth falling open in shock. "You do?"

He nodded, his lashes lowering as he turned his gaze to the ground. He bit down on his lip uncertainly. "Yeah. I think I've been falling for a while, but I only put two and two together when I had the conversation with my mum."

"Liam." I spoke urgently, suddenly needing to let him know that he wasn't alone in this. When he raised his gaze back to mine, I pulled him closer. "I love you too. Fuck. *I love you*. I've been wanting to tell you, but I was worried it was too soon."

He stared at me, his eyes wide and bright, and fuck, I loved him so much. "You do?"

"I do."

He kissed me again, and everything was good.

LIAM

EPILOGUE

FIVE YEARS LATER

At the sound of keys in the lock, a huge grin spread over my face. It widened when the door swung open and Noah stepped into our flat, a bottle of wine and a garlic baguette clasped under his arm.

He crossed the lounge to kiss me, his trainers squeaking a little on the wooden floorboards. "I managed to get the last garlic bread in the shop, and I couldn't remember which wine we had last time, so I got this one because it was on offer. Bloody London prices—even after all this time, I'm still not used to them."

I returned his kiss, then relieved him of his supplies. "You'll get used to them one day. Anyway, the prices where your family live are just as bad. When Layla and Ami asked me to get that Prosecco for their eighteenth birthdays, I nearly fucking passed out when I saw the cost."

"You did not."

"I could've done." Leaning forwards, I gave him another quick kiss. "Pasta's almost ready."

Shrugging off his jacket, he followed me into the kitchen. "I guess you want me to put the garlic bread in the oven, so you can stare at my ass when I bend over."

"Me? I don't need an excuse to look. Or to touch, for that matter." I placed the wine and garlic bread on the counter, then wrapped my arms around him, sliding my hands down to palm his ass. He buried his face in my neck, placing kisses to my throat

"Noah. Fuck." I backed him into the counter, grinding my hips into his.

"Mmm...Liam...we need to wait until we've eaten." His voice was breathless and his pupils were blown when he raised his head to look at me. "But maybe one kiss first."

Angling my head, I brushed my lips across his. "Yeah. One kiss."

Eating incredibly overcooked pasta with no garlic bread because you were too busy kissing the fuck out of the love of your life to focus on mundane things like cooking times? Totally worth it.

When we'd finished eating and I was loading the dishwasher, Noah disappeared. He returned a few minutes later with a couple of photos in his hand. "Look. Preston and Kian sent us these. Preston found them when he was going through some old photos. I thought we could add them to the fridge."

I studied the images as Noah began to move around the photos on the fridge to create a space. We'd covered it in pictures. Me, Noah, and Noah's family, taken at Noah's graduation. My mum and her husband, Geoff, with me at my graduation. An action shot of me in the process of scoring a goal in an LSU championship match—taken by Noah. The two of us in front of the Colosseum in Rome.

Other photos of our friends and the two of us. Memories we'd built together.

There was also a photo of me with my dad on the beach, a copy of the one I had in my bedroom at my mum's house. I smiled, knowing with certainty that he'd be proud of me.

"Remember that night?" Finished with rearranging the pictures to his liking, Noah came up beside me and slipped his arm around my waist. We both looked down at the photos in my hand. "That was the first time I'd seen you in a suit, and you looked so fucking hot. You took my breath away."

"You looked so hot it should be illegal," I informed him, and he huffed out a laugh before placing a soft kiss to my cheek.

The first image was one of the LSU football team ready for the university summer ball, all lined up outside doing stupid poses. The second was a candid shot that I guessed either Preston or Kian had taken. I was standing with Noah on the dance floor, my arms around his waist. Noah's head was thrown back, mid-laugh, and I was just staring at him with the biggest grin on my face.

Fuck, I loved him so much.

I traced my finger over the photo, memories flooding through my mind...

After a pre-ball celebration with the rest of the LSU football team, I turned up at Sanctuary, a huge club and bar in south London where the ball was being held. I was meeting Noah here because he'd had a meeting with one of his course lecturers about a potential summer tutoring job earlier. I couldn't wait to see him—I hadn't seen him since around 8:00 a.m. this morning, and that was way too fucking long as far as I was concerned.

Leaning against the long bar, I glanced at myself in the mirrored wall that ran behind the bar, straightening my tie. The dress code was formal, and although some guys had come in tuxedos, plenty were wearing suits like I was. All the football team had come in matching suits, in fact—a deep charcoal with a slightly lighter grey shirt and a tie in sky blue, our team colour. We all had football cufflinks, and almost everyone had polished black loafers, although I noticed that a couple of the guys had managed to sneak in with black trainers, even though it was against the club's dress code.

I took a sip from my beer, turning around to take in the main dance floor area, everything black and midnight blue. Music pumped through the cavernous space, and sweeping lights lit up the bodies filling the dance floor, moving to the beat.

An instinct made the hairs on the back of my neck prickle, and I placed my beer on the polished bar top next to the full bottle I'd purchased alongside my own, then slowly turned to my left, drawing out the moment.

I sucked in a breath as I took in the sight in front of me.

Noah stood there, looking completely fucking gorgeous, his body wrapped in a dark grey suit just a little lighter than mine, with a deep blue tie. His hair was styled perfectly, and he had a wide smile on his beautiful face.

His eyes sparkled in the club lights as he saw me notice him. Then his gaze swept over me, taking in his own leisurely perusal of my body, and his eyes darkened. His tongue darted out to lick his lips, and I *wanted*. To taste, to touch, to have him.

I crooked a finger at him. *Come here*, I mouthed, and he

stepped closer. When he was right in front of me, I slid my hands onto his sides and tugged him the remaining distance. Breathing in his citrus scent, I trailed my nose up the side of his neck to his ear, hearing his breath hitch at my touch.

"Have I ever told you just how fucking sexy you are?" I took his earlobe between my teeth and lightly bit down.

He shivered, his arms coming up to wrap around my shoulders, his fingernails scraping at the back of my neck, creating a chain of goosebumps down my body. "Speak for yourself. My boyfriend is the hottest person here, hands down." His mouth pressed against the side of my face, and then his lips were touching my ear. "All I could think about when I first laid eyes on you in this suit, looking the way you do, was getting you out of it."

"Fuck," I groaned, my cock thickening in my trousers. I wasn't the only one affected either, if the hardness I could feel against me was anything to go by.

He sighed, his warm breath tickling my ear. "We have to wait, though. I guess I need to at least experience *some* of my first uni ball, especially with those ticket prices."

I nodded, forcing myself to take a step back. He was right, and I didn't want to deprive him of anything. Noah deserved the world, and I'd give it to him.

"Come on." After picking up our beers and passing the full one to him, I took hold of his hand, pulling him in the direction of the dance floor. "Let's drink, and dance, and then when you've had enough, we'll go home and make the most of our alone time."

"Okay. Yeah." Another smile curved over his lips, and I couldn't help kissing him. We eventually found ourselves on the dance floor, caught up in the seething mass of dancers. Downing our drinks, we let ourselves get caught up in the celebratory mood, surrounded by students who were all excited to be finished with a year at university, with a whole summer stretching ahead before the new semester began in September.

We got lost in dancing and hanging out with our friends, but eventually I had enough. I wanted to get Noah alone. Taking his hand, I tugged him towards the edge of the dance floor.

"How did the talk with your lecturer go?" I grabbed the back of his neck, pulling him to me so that he could hear my words.

"He said I had a job if I wanted it." Noah gripped my biceps, pressing against me. "So I guess that means I'm staying here for the whole summer."

"Yeah? You know I'm staying here too." I tried to make my voice casual.

"That was the main incentive for the job." He slid his hands down my arms to wind them around my waist. "An entire summer with you, with just a couple of hours of work tutoring here and there."

"I like the sound of that. A lot." Running my teeth down his throat, I bit down on the tendon in his neck, then began to suck, marking him up so that everyone could see that he was mine.

"Mmm. Liam. Fuck. So good," he breathed. "Me too."

The music changed to a grinding, dirty beat, and our bodies slid together in a rhythm that made my cock so hard, I didn't know how much longer I could last without dragging him somewhere and ripping off his clothes.

Thank fuck he was on the same page as me because he ground himself into me, kissing me fiercely. "I've had enough of this student experience," he moaned in between kisses. "Let's go home."

I didn't need to hear anything else. Gripping his hand

tightly, I dragged him off the dance floor, and he came willingly.

Noah took the photos from my hand and carefully placed them on the fridge with the others. When he turned back to me, his gaze was heated. "Remember how the night ended?"

I groaned, my cock hardening in my jeans at the thought. "Fuck, yeah."

"You wanna re-enact it?" He stepped closer.

Instead of replying, I pulled him to me, and my mouth came down on his.

After all this time together, we were still just as affected by each other as we had been at the beginning. Except now, what we had was so much more special because we had love, and that love got deeper every day.

When we made it to our bedroom, we took our time stripping each other down until there was nothing between us. Face to face, our breaths mingling, he sank inside me until I was full of him, and he was all that I saw.

"I love you," he breathed, lowering his head to kiss me.

I wrapped my arms around him. It took me a second to reply because I was so fucking overcome, completely lost in him, but eventually, I spoke the words that I knew I'd never get tired of saying.

"I love you too."

I always would.

Later, when we were curled around each other, sleepy and sated, Noah raised his head from my chest to meet my gaze. "Want to watch *Attack on Titan*?"

"Again?" I raised a brow at him, amused, as I slid my fingers through his hair. "Go on, then."

His instant smile was so soft and so fucking happy.

Swallowing around the lump in my throat, I moved my hand down to grip his jaw, brushing my thumb over his lips. "But first, I think you need to kiss me."

"Mmm. I think so too." Shifting up the bed, he lowered his head to mine, and I smiled.

THE END

THANK YOU

Thank you so much for reading Liam and Noah's story!

Feel free to send me your thoughts, and reviews are always very appreciated ♥ You can find me in my Facebook group Becca's Book Bar if you want to connect, or sign up to my newsletter to stay up to date with all the latest info. Check out all my links at: https://linktr.ee/authorbeccasteele

Are you interested in reading more from some of the other characters? Check out the following:
    Cross the Line (Kian & Preston)
    Savage Rivals (Asher & Levi)
    Heatwave (Travis & Kira - M/F short story)

Becca xoxo

ACKNOWLEDGMENTS

I couldn't have written this book without the help of some amazing people. Thanks first of all to my uni friends & experiences for inspiring some of the events in the book. And of course to the city of London (is it weird to thank a city? Probably, but hey, I'm doing it) for all the locations that appear in the book. Side note - I definitely recommend checking out the Sky Garden, especially at sunrise!

A biiiiig thank you to Corina and Jenny, who ended up reading 5 million drafts, and had to deal with my dramatics when I was stressing out badly! You're awesome! Thank you to my amazing blogger and ARC teams, to Wordsmith and GRR, and to the bloggers & bookstagrammers - I love and appreciate all the reads, reviews, promo, edits etc. An extra special thanks has to go to my dino-loving friend Claudia for being my biggest support. I love you!

Sandra and Rumi - as usual you had to deal with me being all last minute. I will never change, and I love that you still work with me even so.

Finally, thank you so much for taking the time to pick up this book and read Liam and Noah's story. LSU will be back!

Becca xoxo

ALSO BY BECCA STEELE

M/M Standalones

Cross the Line

Savage Rivals

Blindsided

LSU Series

Blindsided (M/M)

The Four Series

The Lies We Tell

The Secrets We Hide

The Havoc We Wreak

*A Cavendish Christmas (free short story)**

The Fight In Us

The Bonds We Break

Alstone High Standalones

Trick Me Twice

Cross the Line (M/M)

*In a Week (free short story)**

Savage Rivals (M/M)

London Players Series

The Offer

London Suits Series

The Deal

The Truce

The Wish (a festive short story)*

Other Standalones

Mayhem (a Four series spinoff)*

Heatwave (a summer short story)*

Boneyard Kings Series (with C. Lymari)

Merciless Kings (RH)

Vicious Queen (RH)

Ruthless Kingdom (RH)

Box Sets

Caiden & Winter trilogy

(The Four series books 1-3)

**all free short stories and bonus scenes are available from https://
authorbeccasteele.com*

**Key - M/M = Male/Male (gay) romance

RH = Reverse Harem (one woman & 3+ men) romance

ABOUT THE AUTHOR

Becca Steele is a USA Today and Wall Street Journal bestselling romance author. She currently lives in the south of England with a whole horde of characters that reside inside her head.

When she's not writing, you can find her reading or watching Netflix, usually with a glass of wine in hand. Failing that, she'll be online hunting for memes, or wasting time making her 500th Spotify playlist.

Join Becca's Facebook reader group Becca's Book Bar, sign up to her mailing list, or find her via the following links:

facebook.com/authorbeccasteele

instagram.com/authorbeccasteele

bookbub.com/profile/becca-steele

goodreads.com/authorbeccasteele

Made in the USA
Middletown, DE
22 August 2024

59604714R00179